HABITAT

HABITAT

CASE Q. KERNS

BLACK LAWRENCE PRESS

Black Lawrence Press

Executive Editor: Diane Goettel
Cover Art: "Ghost Summer" by Jenna Barton
Book Cover and Interior Design: Zoe Norvell

ISBN: 978-1-62557-163-2

Published 2025 by Black Lawrence Press.
Printed in the United States.

For Sarah & Stella

TABLE OF CONTENTS

Said the condor to the praying mantis,
'we're gonna lose this place just like we lost Atlantis.'
-Neil Young, "Like an Inca"

PART I

THE MAN
WHO KNEW
THE
COLLAGE

"HE'S GONE TOO far this time," Mrs. Farragut said as she entered the ballroom. "It's hideous."

Mr. Farragut walked into the room behind her, reading emails on his phone, his long, narrow frame hunching toward the screen as though his spinal cord was a fishing rod. He was wearing one of his weekend outfits—cotton slacks, a linen button-down shirt, and light brown ostrich-skin loafers without socks. His August Mast cologne announced him whenever he entered a room.

It was the day of the annual Montgomery & Patricia Farragut Summer Gala. I was setting up the bar in the corner of the ballroom and Mrs. Farragut walked over, handing me a small floral arrangement to place next to the ice and prosecco. Mostly, I supervise the rest of the staff and manage the grounds, which wasn't the career path I'd imagined when I was in grad school for urban planning. But after the Crash this was the best job I could get. At least I'm in charge of things. Except during the Gala days when I'm expected to be "in the trenches" as Mrs. Farragut would say.

"Mrs. Farragut," I said, "would you like any other decorations on the bar?"

"No," she said. "Let's keep it simple and again, for the last time, please call me Patricia."

I'd been running around all morning trying to make sure everything was just right. The guests always find things to gossip about behind the Farraguts' backs—the same kinds of things the Farraguts say about other people's parties.

"Monty," she said, turning to her husband. "Edward is your son, too. Some input would be nice."

"I think he's spoiled and lazy," he said to her, lifting his eyes but not his head. "A rebel without any real conflict in his life. The best approach is to ignore his antics and, eventually, he'll regret them."

"That's your solution for our son?" she responded. "Regret?"

"Hector," Mr. Farragut said, bringing me into the conversation. "You're a father. How would you handle this?"

"I have two daughters," I answered, wishing they'd take the argument to another room.

"Right," he said, casually walking over to me and leaning in—another few inches and our foreheads would be touching. "Hypothetically, then."

I had much to say about Edward.

"Leave him alone," Patricia interjected. "If you don't want to talk about Edward with me, then just don't."

"As you wish, dear," he said, letting his eyes fall back down to the screen as he turned away. He didn't seem at all bothered.

"Hector," Patricia said. "The bar looks perfect. Thank you." She gave me a warm smile.

Mr. Farragut stayed behind for a moment after she left the room. He lifted his eyes to meet mine, but his thumb kept swiping. "Make sure the tub on top of the bar is clean before you put ice in it," he said.

I've been the family's estate manager for over twenty years and have always felt a special fondness for Edward, like an uncle for his nephew. Ana tells me there's something wrong with the Farraguts and I should keep my head down and not get concerned with their troubles. We have our own children to worry about. But I've spent so much time with that family, the line between business and personal gets blurry.

Edward was vain from a young age. He didn't think he was better than everybody else like his brother and sister, he just wanted to look and dress a certain way. He had his mother's dark brown hair and her skin that wasn't as pale as her husband's. She was half Italian and half Scottish. Thomas and Ophelia looked more like their father and he preferred them.

Adolescence was much harder for Edward than his siblings. He had to wear braces and his face was riddled with acne. He wasn't cruel about other people's flaws, but he did break a few mirrors after looking at his own reflection. Patricia felt terrible the time I cut myself on glass cleaning up after him. Later, Edward said he'd help me with some of my duties for the next month to make up for it. He even told me once he wished I was his father.

When I got home that night Ana cleaned my cut. She said we couldn't afford for me to be out of work too long if the wound got infected and that I shouldn't have driven across town with an injured hand. I swore Patricia would make sure we were taken care of if I was disabled on the job, but Ana had her doubts.

"She likes you when you make her life easier," Ana said as she poured disinfectant over my wound. "She won't be so generous when you don't."

Edward changed during high school; he was angrier. It was mostly directed at his family and the unfairness of the world. But as much as I agreed with some of his convictions, there was more to it than politics

Toward the end of high school, he started pulling pranks at the annual Gala. He was seventeen the first time, when he streaked naked throughout the party wearing nothing but an elephant mask and a red bow tie. It was funny, but a little over the top. Patricia cried for a long time after everybody left, which made Edward uncomfortable. He'd only really wanted to upset his father and siblings. But his guilt subsided and the pranks continued.

One year he wore a long blonde wig and a gown with makeup and jewelry and even shaved his legs. He flirted with his father's drunk business associates. A few of them flirted back, thinking he was the Farraguts' daughter.

Patricia was always upset by his antics, asking nobody in particular what would make him want to embarrass her like that. Mr. Farragut would call him a jobless leech and cut off his allowance. Thomas and Ophelia despised their brother. When Edward was twenty, they bound and gagged him and left him in the attic during the Gala. They would have let him stay there until morning, but two guests who had snuck up for a secret rendezvous untied him.

Edward told me all about it the next day. He was crying and laughing; I'd never seen him so distraught. He sat at the foot of his bed rubbing the rope marks on his wrists.

"They would have left me there forever," he said.

I put a hand on his shoulder to comfort him, but he jerked away from me.

"I was tied up in the attic for six hours," he said, as angry as he'd ever been.

"We'd have searched for you after it was over," I said.

"You and my mom maybe," he said.

"Your family doesn't hate you, Edward," I said to him as I sat down and put my arm around him. "They just don't necessarily like you all the time, and that's just how it is with blood."

"My father laughed," he said.

Patricia's sister, Catherine, came over to the house early in the hours leading up to this year's Gala. Catherine's a good person who means well, but I find her difficult sometimes. She always wants me to talk about my heritage, asking me the difference between the Spanish my family spoke in Mexico and the Spanish Ana's family speaks in Puerto Rico, even though I told her that all my grandparents were born in Los Angeles, and I didn't learn Spanish until Ana was pregnant. She wanted our children to speak at least three languages.

"Edward will grow out of it," Catherine said, sipping at her tea. "He's a Sagittarius. He's not done traveling yet."

"He's twenty-nine," Patricia responded. "I'm not saying he should become Thomas and Ophelia overnight or even that I'd ever want that, but it's becoming harder and harder to take."

"I know, Tricia," Catherine said. "But he's your favorite."

"Cath," Patricia said quietly but firmly, "don't ever say that. And it's not true, I don't have a favorite."

"Yes, you do," Catherine said, looking at me and shaking her head. "And everybody knows it. Even the Japanese maple in the backyard knows it."

I laughed a little. Catherine could be funny.

"Can we please not change the subject?" Patricia said. "Have you seen it?"

"Seen what?" Catherine asked.

"You won't be so casual about it when you do," Patricia said "It's getting worse."

"Hector," Catherine said, turning to me. "Have you seen it?"

"Yes," I said.

"And?" She asked.

"It's different from the rest."

———————

The first accident was devastating to Edward. He was twenty-four and had just dropped out of a graduate program in media studies. He was standing on a street corner when a motorcycle swerved to avoid hitting a child and went over the curb, crushing Edward's right arm against a building. The rider suffered a broken collar bone, four cracked ribs, two broken legs, and a concussion. Edward's arm had to be amputated. A foot to the right and he would have died. It was a miracle he didn't, but you couldn't say that to him at the time. I'm ruined, he'd say.

For six months he never left the estate. Edward had always been a social animal; he loved being a man about town, and for him to retreat from public life was to give up on existence. Patricia was beside herself worrying about him, and Mr. Farragut preferred it when he wasn't around. They set up consultations on cloning a replacement arm, but he wouldn't go, coming up with an excuse or hiding somewhere until it was too late. They argued that he'd be just like his old self if he consented to the procedure. It would be his arm, cloned from his own DNA.

"It would be a lie," Edward once said to me after an argument with his parents. "It would be the arm of someone identical to me who was never given a chance to live. My arm, but also not my arm."

"You'd have two arms," I said. "Don't you want two arms?"

"Yeah," he answered. "But not like that."

"The only other option would be a transplant from a living donor," I responded. "And that definitely wouldn't be your arm."

Edward went silent, but he had a curious look on his face. I didn't say anything.

"With a transplant, at least the donor would have a choice to give it up and I'd always know it wasn't my arm. There'd be no confusion," he said to me. "It would be like using a fork. I'd have no expectations of it beyond the task at hand." Edward smiled at his pun.

"You need to decide for yourself how to get on with your life," I said.

He began researching transplant surgeries. After a week, he moved from reading articles to watching videos of procedures. He joined online communities, chatting with donors and recipients. We all thought he was emerging from the darkness. His sudden optimism felt like a rebirth.

But soon the types of communities he was engaging with shifted. He started using terms like self-evolution and anatomical autobiography. He became a member of a group called the Phoenix Club.

He began to plaster the walls of his room with pictures of his head combined with a different torso and legs and arms from different bodies, sometimes of other animals. One had his three-year-old head, the upper body of an adult male model in a tuxedo, the naked arms of a bodybuilder, and the lower body of a palomino horse. Underneath it was the title, "Exotic-dancing Equine Edward." The earlier pieces he put together were all like that, weird and crude and playful. They were funny. But the more they covered the walls of his room, the more realistic they became. The animal parts disappeared and were replaced by human body parts that were from different bodies but just about the right size to make up an anatomically balanced person.

Then, one day, he came into the kitchen and told his mother he wanted a transplanted arm instead of a clone. She was so happy to see that Edward was ready to move forward with his life that she didn't question it. Two months later he had a new arm.

Once he fully healed he started leaving the house again, but his social habits had changed. He always went out with other members of the Phoenix Club; they called themselves an "organic exhibit." They'd all had at least one transplant surgery; some had two or three.

"That's some kind of fucked-up body cult," Ana said one night after we'd put the girls to bed. "I know we need you to keep that job, but you have to put up some boundaries. You're too close to him. Let the Farraguts deal with his Frankenstein bullshit."

"I can't just ignore him," I said, as we sat on a couch to watch a show on our laptop.

"You could avoid him. There's a difference between ignoring people and not always making yourself available to them."

"I'll be careful."

"You'll be you," she said, resting her head on my shoulder.

The Phoenix Club homepage, with its logo of a bird rising from a fire, was on our laptop. This bird was made up of many parts, all taken from different species: the crest of a cardinal, an oriole's head, a toucan's beak, a red-tailed hawk's body, an Andean condor's wings, and the talons of a harpy eagle. It was hideous and magnificent.
"If he runs around with them much longer," Ana said as she started to doze off, "he'll want another transplant. It's the next logical step."

———

Catherine found me in the study an hour before guests were due to arrive. I was making some final touches for the Gala. Mr. Farragut had asked for the study to be, in his words, "raggedly presentable."

He wanted to be able to pour a few glasses of a rare scotch or cognac for some VIPs, away from the rest of the party, in a secluded space that looked as if it had not been prepared for use. He told me a spontaneous and private venue makes people feel special and only requires a couple of small details to make it appear authentic. An unfinished cup of black coffee neatly placed next to an open book on top of the desk with the reading light left on—that kind of thing. He usually took cream in his coffee, but the sour odor of dairy sitting for too long could make the atmosphere of the room unpleasant.

Patricia had sent her sister to ask if I'd seen Edward and when I answered no she left without a word to look for him.

Edward's second accident involved the lawnmower. In the hospital afterwards, he said he just wanted to help around the house. He knew how difficult his period of seclusion had been on everybody and mowing the lawn seemed a nice gesture, an olive branch. There was a full-time gardener, so helping with other household chores would have been more useful, but no one loses a hand mopping floors or dusting shelves. Edward wasn't as depressed as he'd been when he lost his right arm. A month later, he had a new left hand.

Patricia tried to pretend it was unintentional, consoling Edward and waiting on him as he recuperated, and he pretended back. Nobody else talked about it, but we didn't have to. Marianna, who had been the Farragut's cook for 25 years, quit suddenly without notice. Even Mr. Farragut seemed upset, and he was never one to pay much attention to what Edward did or didn't do.

When the bandages came off and Patricia saw Edward's new hand, she was furious.

"What did they do to you?" she yelled. "Look at those scars. For the money we paid them, we shouldn't be able to see any at all."

"Mom," Edward said, calmly.

"Don't worry, sweetie," she said. "They'll fix this, or they'll never practice medicine again."

"Mom," he said. "I asked them not to blend away the scars. I asked them to leave them as they are."

"What?" she said. The look on Patricia's face was one I'd never seen before.

"Mom," Edward said again. "Are you okay?"

She picked up a quilt that had fallen onto the floor of his bedroom and folded it twice, laying it neatly along the foot of his bed. She paused for a moment, and then walked out without another word.

Edward turned away from me. It was the first time I saw the tattoo of the Phoenix Club logo on his upper back.

"He's changing," Ana said when we were in bed that night. "You know you won't be able to fix him, right?"

"So, you're saying there's no hope for him?" I said, aggravated.

"I don't even know what that means," she said. "All I'm saying is maybe you should learn to like the phoenix because it's here to stay."

Ana was right. A year after the second accident, there was a third. This time, it involved a table saw and his right hand. We could all see it coming once he started taking woodworking classes.

Even Patricia couldn't pretend any more. She sent him to therapists, a recovery program, but it made no difference. Every one of them concluded that Edward seemed happy and emotionally stable, aside from the intentional amputations and transplants. One even asked if he could include Edward as part of a case study for his new research project. Patricia told him to leave.

Two hours into the Gala, the dinner buffet was open for business and most of the guests were loosened up with three or four drinks. The spread was more decadent than usual: a whole roasted lamb with mint jelly and juniper berry sauce, a dozen jerk-spiced rotisserie chickens, two suckling pigs, a mezze platter station with dips, olives, grape leaves, falafel, and pitas, a table with cheeses, charcuterie, pâtés, and breads from Italy and France, roasted vegetables, sushi, dumplings, udon noodles, and a thirty-foot raw bar. It didn't all go together but the point was extravagance not consistency.

Patricia held court at one end of the ballroom. She was on her second glass of prosecco and only nibbled enough food to keep sober. Catherine stayed by her side, though she was already on her fourth glass. Mr. Farragut was more socially nomadic, moving from circle to circle, laughing at bad jokes and trying to siphon off insider information. Thomas and Ophelia kept looking for their brother, which made me think they had a plan of their own. I once told Ana that I thought they had it in them to kill Edward. She said a lot of people have it in them to murder, depending on what they felt was at stake. I told her it wasn't just that they could undoubtedly do it but that they'd probably feel fine about it after.

Suddenly, the lights went out. The laughter and talking quieted and the voice of a man in a British accent came through the loudspeakers. It was familiar to me, a line of dialogue from a movie. It was Claude Rains speaking.

The dialogue was followed by the sound of a person blowing as if they'd extinguished a birthday candle and then a video projection covered the far wall of the ballroom. It was footage of a desert horizon in the dim orange twilight before dawn. The upper edge of the Sun began to emerge from the horizon to the rising sounds of an orchestra. This faded into a wide-angle shot of the desert in daylight as the theme of *Lawrence of Arabia* began. It had been my late father's favorite film. I had introduced it to Edward when he was fifteen and we had watched it every year on my father's birthday.

Two miniscule figures approached from behind one of the large sand dunes: two men on camels, projected onto the French doors leading out to the backyard. A spotlight illuminated the entrance and Edward entered dressed as Lawrence, wearing a tunic, keffiyeh, and agal. He moved to the center and the spotlight followed him. About a dozen young men and women, all dressed as if they were extras from the film, some with visible transplant scars, emerged from the crowd and danced around him as he slowly rotated in place like a model on a catwalk. The theme song ended and began again. The dancers all kneeled, forming a circle around Edward.

Slowly he took off the headdress to reveal bandages wrapped around his head. Then he carefully removed the bandages and the patch of gauze covering his right ear to show off his newest transplant. The stitches were fresh and slathered with translucent ointment. The new ear was considerably larger and rosier than its match, with a large, puffy, dangling lobe.

Revolving one last time, Edward took a long and graceful bow. His collaborators gave him a standing ovation.

The lights came back on and I looked around to see how the family was reacting. Mr. Farragut quickly recovered and turned to face the group he'd been talking to. Thomas and Ophelia looked furious and left the ballroom. Catherine was as pale as I'd ever seen her. Patricia had a frozen smile and was trying not to cry. Edward was standing still, holding his pose and watching his father. The silence broke and the guests turned back to the food, discussing the spectacle they'd just witnessed.

I walked over to Edward, not knowing whether I was hurt that he'd incorporated the film into his performance or honored it had made such an impression. He looked at me and put his hand on my shoulder, smiling in what seemed a gesture of sincere warmth.

"I'd rather be a lion tamer than a clown," he said, teasing me with a misquoted line from the film. "But, someday, I'll have a tail, Hector, and I'll wag it for the world to see. And then, I'll eat them all."

POTLUCK
BARBECUE

WHILE THE STARTER briquette heated up on the spark-rod, Jared thought about the old fire grills. His family had both charcoal and gas grills throughout his childhood, but he'd opted for gas only when he first lived on his own after college. His father would tell him gas was fine for most things, but to get a good slow smoke with pork shoulder there was no substitute for charcoal with wood chips, which meant patience in tending the fire to make sure it maintained a low and steady heat. Never overfeed it, his father would insist. The first no-flame units started showing up around the time Jared and Wendy moved in together. Two years later, they were so sick of hearing arguments from friends on the culinary and ecological benefits of cooking over a flame-free grill, they gave in and bought one.

Jared missed watching the fire. There were no flames anymore, just glowing. The new briquettes had been introduced to coincide with the unveiling of the no-flame grills. The range and duration of possible temperatures were determined by the size and grade of the briquette and could be controlled through settings on the spark-rod. The whole process was called pyro-incandescence, though it had taken on the nickname "glow-heat." There were explanations and corporate-funded research on this reaction and how it generated such high levels of heat, but these studies were confusing to the layman. The briquettes were made with a mineral called Poseidenium, named after the Greek god because it was discovered on the walls of chasms deep in the ocean, though none but scientists on the payroll of the two corporations that produced the briquettes had ever seen the mineral in nature. Jared's best friend Donnie called them Mars Bars and wouldn't get within twenty feet of one after it had been activated. He was convinced they would eventually give everybody cancer. Jared wasn't sure whether or not they were safe or radioactive, but he missed the fire.

After the last barbecue, it was decided Donnie wouldn't be attending any others, not with the neighbors present. He was a contrarian and Wendy worried it would cause a rift between their family and the rest of the neighborhood; she was terrified that any conflict, no matter how subtle, would negatively impact Amelia and Abe—personal references were so important to landing a good sponsorship. Their whole family's social conduct would be taken into account for the Personality evaluation, which along with Aptitude and Learnedness was one of three criteria virtues which composed the educational sponsorship application process administered by all participating businesses and organizations. The methods used to evaluate and judge each of the criteria virtues varied from employer to employer and between the different tiers of sponsorship, but the three categories always remained the same. Rarely did employers provide any information about their individualized evaluation process to applicants—almost never for tier one sponsorships.

Once both children were placed in schools, the Fong-Stones could lighten up a little and not worry so much about the social consequences of their actions. Abe would be of age in another two and a half years and after they went through the process with him, good or bad, it would be out of their hands. The future would be decided.

Jared clutched the bronze pendant hanging down from his neck, rubbing it between his thumb and forefinger. It had a trunk-like body spreading out into a roughly elliptical head. But what really gave it the appearance of a tree were the designs cut out from the head to look like bare branches, as if in winter after the leaves have fallen. He looked over to the cellar entrance and remembered the last conversation he ever had with his father. "You must tend to the wine cellar after I'm gone," his father had said. "It's important that someone watch over the collection." Jared told his father he had no interest in taking up the Stone family torch. His father told him he had to; it was his duty. Six days later his father died. Jared inherited everything—the house, the property it sat on, and all it contained.

The chicken had been marinating in oil, parsley, onions, and ras el hanout long enough. It was time to assemble the kebabs. Jared had already formed the chickpea mixture into patties, so once all of the guests arrived, everything would be ready to go on the grill. It reflected well on them to have the meal go seamlessly, not making the guests wait and never drawing attention to the effort involved in putting the meal together. Wendy set the table and put out the side dishes to go with the kebabs and patties, having carefully selected recipes that would taste good but not outshine their guests' contributions. Hosting a potluck was such a delicate balance in their neighborhood. Keeping things simple was best so if a dish turned out better than anybody else's one could always self-deprecate culinary skill by pointing out that the ingredients did all of the work. Wendy made a basic tabbouleh, a mixed green salad with olives tossed in lemon vinaigrette, and tzatziki as a condiment. They were all delicious, but she could play them down if necessary.

The Wells-Harrisons were the first to arrive, which was a relief to Jared. He felt he could be himself around them. Freddie and Tanya had moved into the cul-de-sac only five months after Jared and Wendy. Though the neighborhood prided itself on the diversity of its residents, the Wells-Harrisons were the only black family within a one-mile radius. Their daughter Charlene was Amelia's best friend. But, more importantly, they were the only parents Jared and Wendy felt they could speak to openly without worrying it might be used against them. They looked out for each other.

As the adults exchanged greetings, Charlene and Amelia each took one of Abe's arms and guided him off to play House in the small cottage Jared had built for the kids. They were the mommies and he was the baby. It was their favorite game and Abe was just happy not to be abandoned with the adults even though he'd prefer they didn't call him the baby.

Freddie joined Jared at the grill and opened two bottles from the six pack of lager he brought. They raised bottles and each took a sip, then Jared skewered the last of the chicken and onions.

"I was hoping you'd make kebabs," Freddie said, taking another long sip from his beer. He was anxious. "I love those things."

"Is everything okay?" Jared asked.

"Yeah," Freddie said, taking another sip, leaving less than half a beer. "It's fine. It is. Yeah. It's fine."

"Are you sure?" Jared asked.

Freddie looked over to see if Tanya and Wendy were within earshot or paying attention. "Honestly, I've had it with this world, Jared. Had it. It's fucked. Tanya and I have always wanted two or three kids, but now I don't even know if we'll be able to get Charlene into anything above a tier three sponsorship. They expect us to get on our knees and kiss their feet, and all so Charlene can have some bullshit remedial education that will lead her to a life working for the offspring of soulless shits like the Bakers."

"Quiet down," Jared said, wanting to voice his solidarity, but not enough to make him forget the good graces he had to keep up for his own family's future. Amelia still had three interviews left. "They could arrive at any moment."

"Fuck them," Freddie said. "I'm done."

"Freddie!" Jared said. "You guys are still in the running for a few sponsorships. Rant all you want to me or Tanya or Wendy, but you need to look calm. Erratic behavior is a red flag for Personality. Think of Charlene."

Freddie finished his beer, opened another, and immediately drank a third of it.

"You gonna be okay?" Jared asked.

"No," Freddie answered. "But, you're right. I can't just go and give up on Charlene's future before it's decided, which is only another week or two anyway."

When Jared saw both the Hasans and Bakers had arrived, he put the kabobs on the grill, partially to get things rolling and also to avoid walking over to greet them right away. The food couldn't be left unattended. He wouldn't seem rude for staying put. The guests would make their way over, in due time, but they'd make small talk with Wendy and Tanya first. It'd give Jared time to throw back another half of a beer before he'd have to smile and play host. The sound of meat sizzling brought him back. He closed his eyes and pictured flames charring the kebabs with the occasional flare up from fat dripping onto the coals and the grill, caked with greasy residue, catching fire.

———————

The newly-arrived children ran over to the play cottage to join the others, except for the Baker twins who were not yet walking. Asim Hasan, the eldest by fourteen months, talked down to the other children. He'd been sponsored the year earlier and it showed. Tagging closely behind was Thomas Baker who had the confidence of a child more privileged than his neighborhood peers, but he was still terrified and in awe of Asim. He wanted desperately to know what Asim knew and to have seen what Asim had seen, then overtake him. The thirst for blood could be heard in his voice. It made the hairs on the backs of Amelia and Charlene's necks stand up whenever they heard him speak. They called him Thomas Skin-crawl when he wasn't around. Even the way he insisted on being called Thomas and not Tom or Tommy disturbed them. He was too young to be so formal.

Still, the two girls were sure to be friendly with him and not make him feel excluded. They knew upsetting Thomas or his family could complicate their lives. The Bakers were a vindictive lot and generally resented living in the neighborhood. They could afford better, but when it came to educational sponsorships, being a big fish in a little pond was ideal. So they tolerated the lower station, attending potlucks and birthday parties with magicians. The other families' children, like their parents, bit their tongues and suffered the Bakers, with the exception of Asim. He was confident and sponsored. While his mothers, Sonia and Anita, would have preferred he indulge the Bakers until his unborn sibling secured a sponsorship, Asim was too proud to be submissive and despite the fact that many saw the sponsorships as a form of indenture, Asim saw his tier one as induction into a fraternal order more powerful than the Bakers or any single family. He didn't bully Thomas or explicitly put him down, but he refused to hide his distaste or indifference. To not evoke a response was punishment for Thomas, which is why he tried, tirelessly, to make an impression on Asim, who usually acted as though Thomas was nothing more than a light breeze.

"This game is dumb," Thomas said, looking to Asim for agreement. Asim was looking up to the lowest branch of the tree next to the cottage. He jumped up, grabbed the branch, and began climbing, well aware the branches of the tree were too high for Thomas to reach. As Thomas looked up to Asim, Charlene tickled her fingers up and down her bare arm as code for Thomas Skin-crawl to Amelia. They erupted in laughter.

"What's so funny?" Thomas snapped, defensively.

"So, we were playing house earlier and Charlene put a rubber glove on her head as a crown," Amelia said. "But it looked more like a sad rooster. It was so funny."

"And just now," Charlene cut in. "Amelia was doing a chicken dance like she was me earlier. What do you want to be, Thomas?"

"You're so dumb," he said, turning away.

She wanted badly to kick him in the shin, maybe break the skin enough to cause a trickle of blood. Nothing too serious. But Charlene held back her anger because good references weren't as important for Thomas as they were for her and Amelia. His father's money allowed him more leeway in his behavior. He didn't have to worry as much about Personality as the other two criteria virtues. His family would be able to pay for a portion of his education.

"Hey Thomas," Asim yelled from the tree. "Climb up here with me. The view's awesome. I can see your house."

"Maybe later," Thomas said, humiliated. "I need to get something to drink. I'm really thirsty."

He walked off to the buffet table, feeling small and resentful. The rest of the children enjoyed watching his retreat. By the time Thomas reached the beverages, Asim had climbed back down to the ground. Charlene and Amelia returned to their imaginary family.

"He's right," Asim said to them. "This game is dumb."

———————————

Franklin Baker walked over to Jared and Freddie by the grill. They'd just opened the last two beers from the six-pack Freddie brought. Franklin scrutinized the surroundings like a housing inspector.

"I love your old grill, Jared," Franklin said. "That's one of the early no-flame models, right? It's so…vintage. Hello, Fred. How are you?"

"Still breathing," Freddie answered. "You?"

"I can't complain," Franklin said, smugly. "It looks as though Thomas has secured the district tier one spot with CSG, which will provide him with several career options: engineering, legal, computer science, or even executive-track. We couldn't be happier."

Jared wanted to press Franklin's face to the grill. Jared and Wendy had been hoping Amelia would get the Chang Smith Global tier one spot and had spent the past several evenings preparing her for the interview. There was a mutual agreement throughout the cul-de-sac that no two families would apply for the same sponsorship spot in a given year. The Bakers were the only family who hadn't made known where they were taking Thomas for interviews and it had been a growing concern they would compete for spots others had already claimed. Not only was this Jared and Wendy's top choice for Amelia, it was the only tier one sponsorship left among the companies she still had interviews with. Without Chang Smith Global, Amelia's educational path would not be as promising.

Franklin and Susan were taking a sponsorship they had no right to. They were interlopers, pillaging the futures of those less privileged. They were cheating and would never be punished for it.

They had so many options for Thomas. It was as if they just wanted to take something away from somebody else. They hated that they'd never be the richest or most powerful and took it out on the low middles. They were petty, spiteful creatures. Jared lost himself in the glow of the fake briquettes, unconsciously rubbing the pendant again.

Freddie put his hand on Jared's shoulder and squeezed, letting him know he wasn't the only one who despised Franklin. "When are those kebabs going to be done? I didn't come here for the conversation."

"Just a couple minutes," Jared answered.

"Would anyone like a glass of wine?" Franklin asked.

"No thanks," Freddie said. "Just cracked open this beer."

Freddie spit at the ground when Franklin turned his back to get the wine from the buffet table.

"That man's a pig," Freddie said at a volume only Jared could hear. "Pure swine."

"It's fine," Jared said.

"Fine?" Freddie said. "How can it possibly be fine?"

"I just have to believe things will work out for Amelia," Jared answered.

"So, you're a man of God now?" Freddie asked.

"Let's just call it cosmic faith," Jared said. "Could you grab me a serving platter for the food?"

Freddie went in search of a tray and Franklin came back to the grill with a glass of wine and two deviled eggs on a compostable napkin. He ate one of the eggs, almost slurping it up, and washed it down with wine.

"What kind of wine did you bring?" Jared asked, knowing Franklin was fond of his own wine enthusiasm.

"It's a Nebbiolo," Franklin said. "One of my go-to reds in the summertime."

"You see those storm doors set away from the house?" Jared said, pointing to the entrance in the middle of the yard. "It's the entrance to my wine cellar"

"Really?" Franklin said, suddenly engaged. "I didn't know you were a collector."

"Oh yeah," Jared said. "A hobby I inherited from my father, which he inherited from his. I had no interest in it when I was younger, but since my father died, it's made me feel more connected to him."

"What's the pride of your collection?" Franklin asked.

"I have a bottle of 2010 Monfortino Barolo Riserva," Jared answered.

"How'd you get one?" Franklin asked. "That vintage is impossible to find."

"Dumb luck," Jared said. "Found it at an estate sale. The seller had no idea how valuable it was. I probably didn't pay much more than you did for that Nebbiolo."

"I'd love to see it," Franklin said. It was the first time Jared had seen envy in Franklin's eyes. "The Barolo, but also the whole collection."

"Sure," Jared said. "But I don't really have time right now. Too many guests to entertain."

"I'm sure they wouldn't miss us for a few minutes," Franklin said, eager.

"Why don't you come back later tonight, around 7pm?" Jared said. "Wendy's taking the kids to a movie. We can open a decent bottle and I won't have to rush you."

"I guess I could stop by later," Franklin said, swallowing the second deviled egg in one mouthful and finishing his wine. He wiped his mouth with the napkin, crumpled it up and let it fall from his hand to the ground, ignoring the compost bin five feet away. "I'm going to get some more Nebbiolo."

Jared picked up the crumpled napkin and tossed it in the bin. Freddie returned with the serving platter and two more beers. "What was that all about?"

"Nothing," Jared said. "Just some unpleasant small talk."

"Franklin looked upset," Freddie said, "which is a far cry from his resting victory face."

"Thanks for getting the tray," Jared said, immediately transferring the food from the grill.

"You're not going to say anything else about the exchange you just had?" Freddie said.

"I have a bottle of wine he wants," Jared said. "And he's pissed I wouldn't show it to him."

"Really?" Freddie said.

"Pretty much," Jared said, placing the last of the patties on the tray with a spatula.

"Sweetie," Wendy said to Jared as the guests started to seat themselves. "Could you help me get a few more chairs for the children?"

They walked behind the cottage where the extra folding chairs were leaning against the back wall.

"Jared," she said and started to cry.

"I know," he said, putting his arms around her. "Franklin made an announcement to us by the grill."

"What are we going to do?" she asked. "They could have said something months ago. We could have found some other options.

It's like they wanted to ruin our daughter's life."

"We'll figure this out," Jared said. "CSG hasn't cancelled our interview yet. So let's just go forward with it, and if what the Baker's say is true, we'll find something else for Amelia."

"No, we won't," she said.

"Listen," he said. "I'm not going to let them decide Amelia's future. Okay?"

"Okay," she said, unconvinced by his confidence, but appreciative of the gesture. They grabbed a couple of folding chairs and walked back to the tables.

The children sat together at the shorter table, eating mac & cheese and veggie dogs, which Tanya had brought over in what Wendy would call her typical "life-saver" fashion, lifting the stress of the children's meal off of her shoulders. Tanya also brought a cumin-spiced macaroni salad, which complimented the kebabs and Wendy's sides perfectly. Sonia and Anita brought homemade baklava, made with honey from the bees they kept. The pastries were pristine little triangles, evenly dusted with ground pistachios. Sonia took equal credit though Anita had been up most of the night, alone, crafting several iterations of the dessert until it was just right. Anita didn't challenge her wife's false claim, but she had a slight tic on the right side of her face, which was always more severe when she was stressed and felt unacknowledged. Sonia leaned over, navigating the gravity of her own eight-and-a-half-month pregnant body, and kissed Anita on the cheek, causing the tic to become less exaggerated.

Franklin and Susan brought salmon mousse and a chicken liver pate with crostini, which they hadn't made themselves. Once the adults were seated at the higher table, they tasted and praised all of the dishes. Then Sonia took the floor and said she hoped there wouldn't be another heat wave during the last weeks of her pregnancy—humidity being the one thing she couldn't bear in her present state. Wendy agreed and commiserated with Sonia, relieved the topic of conversation wasn't sponsorship. It was an intentional kindness. Everyone had heard what Franklin and Susan had said about CSG and knew what it meant for Jared and Wendy. Sonia continued to talk about her pregnancy and how much she wanted to get it over with already. Tanya and Wendy nodded in sympathy.

When Franklin arrived that evening at seven on the dot, Jared was alone in the house. Wendy had been gone with the kids for over an hour and wouldn't be back before nine. The neighborhood was quiet. Franklin knocked on the back door and they went directly to the wine cellar entrance. The door had a bolt lock, a padlock, and a keypad to the door handle. Jared obstructed Franklin's view while he punched in the code.

"That's a lot of security," Franklin said. "Do you think you're overdoing it?"

"Maybe," Jared answered, gesturing for Franklin to go first. "But it's a valuable collection, which I can't afford to replace."

"Fair enough," Franklin said as they descended the steps. It was too dark to see what was ahead of him. "You're not going to knock me over the head and wall me up down here, are you?"

"No," Jared said. "I hate manual labor."

Franklin laughed. It was his kind of joke. Jared turned on the lights to reveal a large room with two-and-a-half walls of wine racks, about a quarter of which were filled with bottles, maybe two hundred and fifty in all. Towards the back wall, in the middle of the room, was a large wooden table with two matching chairs. On the table were four wine glasses on top of a woven place mat, an open bottle of wine, a leather-bound notebook, a pen, a wood-handled wine key, and a copper bowl filled with corks.

Hanging on the wall above the table was a wood carving of a tree identical to the pendant Jared wore around his neck. It was a symbol of his family's history—a legacy he'd been trying to outrun his entire life. He always believed if he could break the cycle and abstain, then neither of his children would ever have to wear the pendant. They would be able to enjoy a future unburdened by the customs and responsibilities of the Stone bloodline. They would be free. They were Fong-Stones.

But looking at Franklin standing in front of the wood-carved tree, Jared knew it wasn't his family's history that had taken his daughter's future away from her.

"Why the dirt floor?" Franklin asked, looking down to his feet.

"My grandfather originally intended to build a fallout shelter down here," Jared answered, walking towards the table. "But in the middle of construction, he'd outgrown his paranoia and decided it could be used as a wine cellar instead. To be honest, I like the aesthetic of having a dirt floor. It makes the space seem older, well-aged."

"I see the appeal there," Franklin said, feigning interest, but failing to hide his impatience. "Can I see the Barolo?"

"Of course," Jared said as he picked up a less valuable bottle of Cabernet franc and poured two glasses, handing one to Franklin. "But, first a toast."

"To good vintages," Franklin said and they each took a sip.

Jared put his glass down and then retrieved the bottle. As

promised, he presented a 2010 Monfortino Barolo Riserva. Franklin looked as though he'd just found God.

"I wasn't sure I should believe you earlier," Franklin said. "I can't tell you how long I've been looking for one of these."

"I was beside myself when I found it," Jared said.

"How much?" Franklin asked.

"What?" Jared responded, playing coy.

"For the bottle?"

"It's not for sale," Jared said, firmly.

"How much?" Franklin insisted.

"It's a very special bottle," Jared said, gently taking the bottle from Franklin's hands and placing it upright on the table.

"Name your price."

"I don't really want your money," Jared said.

"What do you want?" Franklin said.

Jared took a moment to make it seem as though he hadn't already planned for this negotiation.

"As you probably know," Jared said, trying to read the level of desire on Franklin's face. "Wendy and I were hoping to land the CSG tier one sponsorship for Amelia. If you were to withdraw Thomas' sponsorship and recommend Amelia in his place, I'll let you have the bottle for free."

"Oh," Franklin responded, never taking his eyes off the bottle. His attention was focused on its label, which was the color of an ancient scroll. "It's a deal."

"You're willing to give up the sponsorship?" Jared said, surprised at how smoothly it had gone.

"Thomas has offers from three other tier one companies," Franklin answered. "They're all just as good as CSG."

"I'll want it in writing," Jared said. He tore a piece of paper from the notebook and placed it on the table, composing the agreement and then signing it. He felt powerful. He wished Freddie had been there to see it—the dethroning of the interloper. He held out the pen for Franklin to add his signature.

"No thanks," Franklin said, repressing a grin.

"What do you mean?" Jared said, bewildered.

"I was just messing with you," Franklin said. "How about five thousand dollars instead?"

"But you just said you'd trade the sponsorship for the bottle."

"Do you really think I'd trade my son's sponsorship slot for a bottle of wine?" Franklin said. "Susan would have my head."

"You said he has three other tier one sponsorships to choose from," Jared said.

"And CSG was our top choice."

Jared felt hollowed out, as if he'd been transformed from organic matter into negative space, his skin the only lingering remnant of his former self. All he could see was Franklin's grin, a Cheshire cat smile that seemed to float alone in the room, disembodied from the rest of him. The voices swiftly occupied Jared's emptiness.

"Are you going to sell me the bottle or not?" Franklin asked.

"It's worth a lot more than five thousand," Jared responded. They were begging him. Hundreds of them. Begging him to blow.

"Yeah," Franklin said. "But that's my final offer and I think we both know you're going to need all the money you can get without a tier one for Amelia."

"Please reconsider," Jared implored. He wanted so desperately for the trade to take place. He'd been so strong resisting the voices for so many years.

"I'll throw in an extra five hundred for that written contract as a memento," Franklin said smiling as he picked up the bottle, admiring its perfect condition.

Jared backed away until the backs of his thighs bumped the table. They were screaming for him to blow. What seemed hundreds now sounded like thousands of voices to him. They were so loud and widespread throughout his head he couldn't hear his own thoughts. To resist them any longer was to choose madness as a way of life.

"I'm sorry," Jared said. "I really wanted things to go the other way."

He grasped the pendant and touched the tip of its trunk to his lips and blew. It was a whistle with a surprisingly low tone and soft like a wooden flute.

"What is that?" Franklin asked.

"Goodbye, Franklin."

Tendrils shot up from the earth, wrapping themselves around Franklin's wrists, ankles, and torso as though he'd been taken hostage in the jungle in an old comic book, bound by his captors with vines. He didn't say anything. The terror was too much to process into words as he tried to break free, but the more he struggled the more the tendrils tightened their grip. He couldn't pull away. He stared into Jared's wide, unblinking eyes as Jared walked over and gently took the bottle from his hands.

Once the tendrils secured him in place, large tentacle-shaped roots slowly rose up from the dirt. There were large thorns on the roots where some squid would have toothed suckers and hooks. When these roots had completely surrounded Franklin as if bars on a cage, they all struck inward at his body, piercing his flesh with the thorns and pulling him down to the ground. He screamed from the pain of the puncture wounds and out of the fear of not just witnessing the unfathomable, but being touched by it. The screams would never leave the wine cellar. Jared had closed the door at the top of the stairs, which was heavy and soundproofed.

Jared sat down at the table and sipped his wine. The voices began to diminish the moment he blew the pendant whistle. Thousands became hundreds became dozens.

Franklin struggled, but it was a useless struggle. He wasn't fighting against an animal or a man. It was an ancient beast made up of the earth itself. There was no beginning or end to its organism, no fixed body. It could command the minerals and rhizomes to do its bidding.

Franklin was slowly pulled under the earth's surface as if the dirt were water.

As Jared watched Franklin's hand vanish into the dirt, the last of the voices went quiet within him. He hadn't realized how constant they had been since his father died, when he started wearing the pendant. As troubling as it was to cross this line, the silence was a relief.

He'd spent so many years standing a moral ground against the ritual of sacrifice. But now that he'd seen the entity and witnessed how powerful it was, he knew it had to be tethered. If it somehow broke free and roamed the Earth's soils without constraint, all of humanity would be at its whim. Jared had no choice but to accept the responsibility his father had passed down to him.

After he finished up in the wine cellar, Jared would call the Baker's house, asking to speak with Franklin. "I thought he was at your house," Susan would say, confused. Jared would tell her Franklin never showed up. She would begin to panic and he would tell her not to worry.

Jared thought about the CSG sponsorship. Without Franklin's income, Thomas would likely lose the spot. The family's future income projection would change drastically, unless Susan found a job with a salary commensurate with Franklin's. This wasn't impossible; she'd received a doctorate in economics and had managed the sponsorship budget for a large corporation before Thomas was born, but she wouldn't be able to find a job before the sponsorship season was over. Their future income projection would not change back until the following season, which would be too late for Thomas.

The question remaining was whether or not Amelia would be first in line for the CSG sponsorship after Thomas. They had no way of finding out how many children were in the running. All they could do was prepare. The interview was two days away.

OUR DAY
WILL COME

THE FIRST STEP was the hardest. All the interior floors and exterior surfaces within the prison grounds were flat and consistent.

Jolene had thought the blast of direct sunlight hitting her in the face as she walked out the East Gate would be the most severe change. The prison yard had always been covered in a blanket of shade for morning recreation. But it was the uneven earth that threw her off. She'd never walked out in the world with only one foot. It didn't help that the prosthetic she'd been provided with inside had been top of the line with proper joint tension and alignment. Some days she'd even forgotten it wasn't real until it was time to shower. The model they let her leave with may have looked like a foot, but it didn't move like a foot.

Her right ankle buckled when the prosthetic touched down on the edge of a shallow pothole and she fell to the ground. She was alone. Her tongue hit straight onto the red dirt, coating her taste buds. A little dust cloud hit the back of her throat. Not wanting to fall again, she crawled five yards to a bench so there would be something to lean on as she stood up.

As she regained her balance, Jolene realized they hadn't provided her with a state-of-the-art prosthetic on the inside for her benefit, but for their own. No one wanted to pick her up off the ground all day.

There were twenty minutes before the first shuttle arrived and she was about two hundred yards from the shuttle-stop. It'd be another three hours until the next. Three hours with no cover under a Southwestern sun. Jolene took up the cane they'd given her, which she'd resisted using at first, and began the slow journey across the unpaved prison parking lot.

––––––––––

When she'd been called into the conference room, Jolene was only six months into a ten-year sentence and had just shaved off all her hair. Not to skin, but to a fine brown stubble. The room looked corporate, unlike any of the spaces where inmates met with visitors or prison officials. It even had a window looking out on the horizon. The kind of space she imagined many of her old clients carried out their takeovers and board meetings in. The man sitting at the table wore a tailored suit and wasn't very good at sitting still, shifting so much in his seat it looked like choreography arranged by a nervous dancer, which meant he probably didn't work in prisons on a daily basis. He looked afraid, like he wanted to get whatever he was there to do over with and get out, which gave Jolene a rare sense of power.

He introduced himself as Rick Toomey, an executive account manager in organic acquisitions at Hippocratium Inc., which he followed up with their corporate motto, "Building the New You!"

"I don't want to take up too much of your time," he said, tone deaf to his surroundings. "So, let's get down to business."

"Why?" Jolene asked.

"What?" He responded.

"Why don't you want to take up too much of my time?" she said. "What difference could it possibly make to me? It's either this or making wampum for a dollar a day."

"It's just an expression," he said, visibly annoyed by her questions.

"I know it's an expression," she said.

Mr. Toomey picked up a manila folder and shuffled through the papers inside to avoid an immediate response. Jolene took the opportunity to look out the window, focusing on the mountains in the distance—a ridge providing a sense of endless nature to the red desert because it blocked out the truck-stop on the other side. None of the windows she normally had access to were facing the mountains.

"You have a ten-year sentence, correct?" he asked.

"I thought I was just here for the weekend," she responded.

He looked at her with the eyes of a man who wouldn't be talked to like that. Not by her. He straightened up his shoulders and smirked to display his confidence.

"And you have a five-year-old daughter, orphaned as a result of your conviction," he said, trying to contain his smile. "You'll be stuck in here no matter what, but the next ten years are vital to her future and an educational sponsorship is unlikely. I want to help you make sure she doesn't suffer for your crimes. Don't you?"

"What are you proposing?" she asked, telling herself no good would come from grabbing his pen and stabbing it through one of his smug little eyeballs, even though she could. Even with the handcuffs on.

"We have an exciting new initiative," he said. "An opportunity allowing inmates like yourself to help improve the lives of loved ones on the outside."

"What is it?"

"A donation program," he said.

"What kind of donation?" She asked.

"A little part of yourself."

"What part?" she asked.

"That depends," he said. "What kind of life do you want to provide for your daughter?"

———————

The shuttle was a sixty-mile ride to town. About the size of a small bus, it seated twenty at most, like a subway car with built-in benches along the sidewalls instead of rows. There were three other passengers already on the shuttle. They all lived in one of the handful of one-road towns near the prison. The shuttle was their only way of getting to the city for their jobs. Most local residents worked at the prison or one of the few businesses nearby, but there was only so much work to go around out there.

A man wearing a Best Buy shirt, at least a size too small for him, sat across from Jolene at a diagonal. He smiled at her, then slowly ogled up and down and back up her body, ending on her eyes and raising a brow to make a silent proposition. She shook her head lazily but firmly and looked out the window. It was a dreadful landscape. Not wondrous like the mountains behind the prison, but flat and without character except for some barbed wire fencing and the wavy blur of heat lines.

"Every day," said the woman sitting next to Jolene in a loud whisper, "I have to watch those slimy eyes of his."

Jolene smiled and nodded her head but offered no words. The woman wore a uniform a woman working at a diner in the 1950s might have worn. At least, that's what they looked like in the movies. It reminded Jolene of one of her old clients who loved making comments like, "They just don't build them like they used to." He was a jackass, but better than most men and lightened up by his childlike nostalgia for a bygone era, which preceded his birth by decades.

As the excitement of being released began to settle, her thoughts shifted to her daughter, Felicia. Jolene took out the only photo she had. It was from Felicia's fifth birthday; three weeks later Jolene was arrested. She tried to imagine what the fifteen-year-old Felicia would look like. Was she tall? What was her hair like? Did she dye it? Were her ears pierced? Did she like boys or girls or both or still neither? Was she happy? Hundreds of questions flooded in, but she had to stop herself so she could focus her energies on finding instead of fantasizing about her daughter. She'd had ten years to wonder.

All she had to go on was what child services would or wouldn't tell her and the name of the agency that facilitated the adoption. She didn't even know the name of the family who adopted Felicia or where they lived, and she had meager resources at her disposal. A decade of labor and Jolene still left the prison with very little money. There was enough for the cross-country bus trip and maybe enough to get by on for a few weeks while she searched for Felicia. But beyond that she had nothing. No home. No job. No possessions to sell. She'd lost everything in the civil suit.

The ogling man in the tight shirt got off at the first shuttle stop and mumbled "prison trash" under his breath as he walked by Jolene, but she barely noticed.

The bus station was the second stop in town. Jolene bought a ticket for a five-day trip to Boston, which only ran once a week. In the few hours she had to kill before her bus left, she went out in search of cheap snacks and something to read. She hadn't the money to buy a digital reader, so she had to settle for whatever musty used print books might be laying around the nearest pawn shop. She found a beat-up hardcover of Roget's Thesaurus and an omnibus of five adventure thrillers, all following the escapades of ex-Rhodes Scholar and motorcycle daredevil turned antiquities collector Stroker Johnson. Jolene laughed out loud at the name. Each book followed Stroker and his chopper to remote locations as he acquired precious treasures and historical artifacts in what seemed a melding of Evil Knievel and Indiana Jones. The idea of losing herself in something as ridiculous as *Stroker Johnson & The Crypt of Golden Fangs* for five days across the country was so appealing she had to have it. Along with the two books, she grabbed a big bag of mixed nuts, a gallon of water, and made her way back to the bus.

Jolene's wampum circle in prison had been made up of seven other mothers and herself. Six of them had "donated" at least one foot. Feet were the most common donation. They reaped some of the largest benefits because their visibility to onlookers made them especially desirable to recipients, and most inmates kept their hands because they were needed for manual labor to make money on the inside.

A woman named Sally B was the only woman in the circle who'd donated both feet. She had four children and a husband who made very little money even though he had two jobs, one as a parking attendant and the other as a graveyard shift security guard. He tried hard, but only made enough to fully support two people. The donation recipient was a young heiress who'd lost both of her feet in a car accident and badly wanted both transplants to come from the same donor. She offered a voucher to fully fund boarding school and college for all four children in exchange for two matching feet. Aside from the six women in the group who'd donated feet, there was Francesca who donated a kidney to get a healthcare voucher for her son, which only covered pediatric primary care and not specialists or surgery—an external donation would have provided full coverage. The last woman was Angie whose husband Sal had landed a job as a foreman for a large construction company with family healthcare and free labor apprenticeships for the children of employees, so she'd avoided making any donations for the time being.

All the women at the prison labored for The Great North American Trading Co., a large conglomerate specializing in recreating objects, both indigenous and colonial, from early American and frontier life. Jolene and her circle made wampum every day from ten in the morning until six with one break for lunch and another brief mid-afternoon coffee break. They'd been mentored to make the wampum as the objects had originally been crafted hundreds of years earlier, using real quahog and whelk shells, shaping them to tubular beads, some kept separate and some strung into patterns as belts. The demand for authentic recreations had grown over the last few decades, but the cost of artisan labor had outstripped what consumers were willing to spend, so prisons became the perfect factory home for the arts and crafts industry. Collectors liked the idea of cultural continuity to the environment in which these objects were created, so Jolene's prison only produced objects of the colonial New England period. They had even renamed her prison The Mayflower Puritan Correctional Facility for Women, located over two thousand miles southwest of the pilgrims' original settlement.

"Pass me the hand drill," Sally B asked. Jolene handed over the stone tool and Sally B set the rounded piece of quahog in place. "You know, there's a reason modern tools exist, and it's because they're better."

"We sit here for just as long and get paid the same whether we produce one or twenty a day," Jolene said, adding a whelk bead to the belt she was making. "Besides, it could be worse. We could've been assigned to the tannery, which would've meant days spent breathing in the odor of corpse skins."

Francesca shuddered and looked at Jolene with disgust.

"Animal corpses," Sally B corrected. "You said it like it could be people."

"Who knows?" Jolene said with a smirk. "Not as many cows as there used to be, but there's still a lot of leather."

"Stop it!" Francesca demanded. "That's vile. Even if you're joking."

"I'm sure the skin comes from people who are already dead," Jolene responded, "and from natural causes, of course."

Sally B tried to suppress her laughter and few of the other women in the circle did the same.

"You're disgusting," Francesca said to Jolene.

They all went back to work in silence to let the mood reset itself. Jolene enjoyed teasing Francesca but didn't want to push her away. She never wanted to make any of the other women feel alone and isolated from the circle. So, she never took it too far.

"What do you think they'll use for wampum beads when all of the clams are gone?" Francesca asked a few minutes later, partially to show she was no longer upset and because she was curious.

"You think all of the clams are going to die?" Sally B asked.

"Don't you?" Francesca responded. "I read that they think the Indochinese Tiger is extinct."

They went quiet again, but not to reset the mood. They were solemn. Tears welled up in Angie's eyes. The running joke was she liked cats more than people.

"If the clams go," Jolene interjected, "we'll probably use people's bones for beads."

Everybody laughed, even Francesca.

When the bus reached South Station in Boston, Jolene was in the middle of revising *Stroker Johnson and the Lost City of the Turquoise Jaguar*. She'd finished the omnibus of adventure novels in the first two days of the trip and though she found them thoroughly entertaining, there was room for improvement. She began heavily revising the novels with a mechanical pencil and Roget's Thesaurus as her tools. She wondered if the author, Tom Jacobson, was still alive and if he'd mind her improvements to his work. Then she wondered if she'd even want his approval.

Once inside the station, she sat at a small table next to a cafe kiosk to collect herself before making her next move. She'd contacted her second cousin Tammy, who told Jolene she could stay with her for the first week, but then she'd have to make her own arrangements.

She'd never met anyone from the agency handling Felicia's adoption because it was all arranged after she went to prison. The social worker from child services who'd handled Felicia's case, a woman named Amy Silva, had been sympathetic towards Jolene. She was really the only one who seemed to think it was a bad idea to split up the mother and daughter. Jolene thought she might be able to guilt Amy into helping her.

Tammy lived in a two-bedroom railroad apartment with her husband Frank and her grown son Frank Jr. She was the only family Jolene had left, beside Felicia. Jolene stopped by to pick up the spare key before she went to find Amy Silva.

"Thank you, Tammy," Jolene said. "I can't tell you how much this means to me."

"Yeah, well, Frank Jr. works nights, so you can sleep in his bed,"

Tammy said, looking like she'd already had enough of Jolene. "But under no circumstances is that room to be used as a place of business. And if you think I won't turn you in because we're family, you're dead wrong."

"I understand," Jolene responded, smiling humbly. "I just want to find my daughter. You'll barely notice I'm here."

"Maybe you shouldn't," Tammy said.

"Shouldn't what?" Jolene asked.

"Maybe she'd be better off if you didn't find her," Tammy said, handing Jolene the spare key and walking away into the kitchen.

———

Jolene sat on a bench in front of the office for the Department of Children and Families. She'd decided to approach Amy Silva outside the office, figuring she would be more likely to follow a hard line on the rules while surrounded by coworkers.

"Amy," Jolene called out as Amy walked by the bench at lunchtime. She walked swiftly, but carefully, as if she were constantly observing each of her steps and movements, triangulating her proximity to objects and her contact with the ground. Her black hair was done up in a bun. She was dressed in a navy-blue business suit and white athletic shoes that clashed with the outfit.

"Yes," Amy said, stopping and turning her head. When she fixed her eyes on Jolene's face, her warmness subsided. "I can't talk to you."

"Please," Jolene said. "I need to find her. Just point me in the right direction."

"I'm sorry," Amy said and continued walking away.

Jolene stood up, using the cane for support, and chased after her at an unsteady limp. Amy was quickly getting away from her.

"Help!" Jolene begged loudly. "Amy!"

Amy looked back and when she saw the cane, she stopped. She didn't mean to. She meant to keep walking, intending to tell herself she couldn't help them all. These confrontations happened often, every week or two. She'd remind herself to move on and focus on her active clients. But, when she caught sight of the cane and then the prosthetic foot, she froze up. It wasn't out of sympathy over the physical handicap. Amy had suffered from brittle bone disease all her life, which left her with little patience for people who let the challenges of their physicality hold them back. There were some exceptions, but it would have to be more than a missing foot.

She stopped because she knew why Jolene was missing a foot. When she received education vouchers for children she was working with, there were no details on the source of the gift, just the amount and what it was allotted for. In most cases, she could put two and two together, especially if one or both parents were in prison. Most prisoners had almost no accumulated wealth. But the confidentiality of the source allowed her to pretend it was something else. Like maybe Jolene had squirreled away a nest egg for Felicia with a trusted associate or a sympathetic client. Or maybe there was a relative who had come into some money.

But the moment she saw the prosthetic, she knew Jolene had traded away her foot for Felicia's education. They'd stolen ten years of her life and then she let them carve off a piece from her own body so her daughter could get a decent education.

"Meet me at Angela's Diner at seven," Amy said and walked away without another word.

Jolene went back to the bench and sat down because it was free, and she wouldn't have to buy anything while she waited. After a few hours, she'd try to find another bench closer to the diner. She opened her bag and took out *Stroker Johnson and the Lost City of the*

Turquoise Jaguar to continue her revision.

_____

Angela's Diner was a landmark but had been reconstructed and revamped so many times there was little left resembling the original establishment except for the font used on the sign and the basic geometric shape, which was similar to the train-car structure of its early days. Every new owner tried to include some remnant of its old aesthetic in the redesign to appease neighborhood nostalgia. Angela's was a symbol of what the area had been and what hadn't changed. But with each reopening, its familiarity diminished and every attempt at a harkening back felt more and more forced. Jolene waited outside until Amy arrived so she wouldn't have to order anything. She'd only budgeted for one coffee a day.

When they sat down in a booth, Amy ordered a piece of Boston cream pie and a cup of coffee. Jolene shook her head to the waiter.

"Are you sure?" Amy asked. "It's on me. I insist."

"Then, I'll have the same," Jolene said.

The waiter wrote down their order and moved on to the next table.

"You can order dinner," Amy said.

"The pie is enough. Thanks," Jolene responded. "Do you have some information for me?"

"If I help you," Amy said, looking around to see who was within earshot, "this can't ever get back to me."

"It won't," Jolene said. "I just want to see her, not steal her away from her new family."

Amy nodded her head and kept silent as the waiter delivered their pie and coffee.

"You should take a trip to Providence before you settle into a new job," Amy said, still looking around. "I used to go down every few months to visit a family I was friends with, the Whartons. We had a bit of a falling out and have lost touch over the last few years. Otherwise, I'd put you in contact with them and ask them to show you around. It's still worth the trip."

Jolene thought Amy's coded delivery of information was unnecessary. Nobody around them cared what they were talking about, but if it helped put Amy at ease, then so be it. She was helping and she didn't have to. Feigning some sort of cloak-and-dagger rendezvous was a small price to pay for the assistance.

"Great idea," Jolene said, enthusiastically. "I haven't been to Providence since I was a child, and I could use a little getaway. Thanks for the suggestion."

"I have to go now," Amy said, having only eaten two bites from her slice of pie.

"Is there any way I can repay you?" Jolene asked.

"Just don't ever contact me again," Amy answered.

"I won't," Jolene said. As Amy walked away, Jolene waved down the waiter and asked for a to-go container. She ate half of her slice and packed up what was left of her slice and Amy's into the container, and then finished both cups of coffee.

––––––––––

Jolene had been left alone in the room for some time after she'd changed into the hospital robe. Sitting upright on the examination table with her leg bent to an A-frame, she stared at her right foot, which lay flat on the tabletop. She was studying it so she could remember. The veins and little hairs. The metatarsal bones pushed out like they wanted to tear through the skin when she lifted her toes up. The callus on top of her hammertoe, hardened by rubbing against her shoe. Her over-trimmed toenails. These were their last moments together.

She was sick to her stomach, but there was no turning back. She'd already signed all the waivers and forms. They could force the amputation against her will and have the legal paper trail to exonerate them of any wrongdoing. Besides, if she backed out at this point, after a wealthy recipient had already been prepared for the transplant, it wouldn't just be a matter of her daughter not receiving an education voucher. Both the recipient and Hippocratium Inc. would make sure Felicia suffered for her mother's withdrawal from their agreement.

It was no longer her foot. It belonged to them. As panicked as she was waiting in the room, her daughter would have a fully-funded education, placing her in higher demand for adoption. Felicia would escape the foster care system, which was priority number one.

Before she was sent to prison, Jolene had saved enough to pay for part of Felicia's education and seek a partial sponsorship for the remaining costs. She'd been smart with her money. She had a plan. But then she was arrested and convicted of prostitution without a license, which meant ten years in prison. The severity of the sentence was to act as a deterrent, plus it was a federal crime since the government regulated and oversaw the escort corporations. Anyone who wasn't a registered employee with one of those four companies was committing an act of conspiracy against the state.

Once she was sentenced, the civil suit began. It didn't last very long. All four escort corporations—Escorp, Red Satin Inc., Sheer Excursions, and The Touch Corporation—were named plaintiffs in the lawsuit, claiming all her earnings as profit losses. If she had worked for one of them, after they had taken their percentage of her earnings and the government had collected her registration and health taxes, there would only be enough left over to modestly support the two of them. Felicia wouldn't have an education fund and the only sponsorship available to her would be for an entertainment apprenticeship with the escort corporation her mother worked for.

In the end, Jolene could provide more for her daughter sitting in prison and letting them take away her foot than if she'd worked for one of the corporations. She could never comprehend the appeal of the donor transplants or why they'd become such status symbols. With all the advances in cloning, someone with that much money could have an organ or appendage grown from their own genetic material. Why would they want someone else's foot or hand when they could have their own?

A surgical assistant and prison guard entered and escorted her on a gurney to the makeshift operating room, which had been set up at one end of the infirmary. The recipient was shielded by a curtain so their identities would remain anonymous to each other. As the surgeon prepared for the transplant, the anesthesiologist began to administer an IV drip through a vein in Jolene's left arm.

She wiggled the toes on her right foot to feel them until she fell out of consciousness.

The name Felicia Wharton was uncommon enough that there was only one in the state of Rhode Island, and all New England, for that matter. The Wharton family still lived in Providence, in the southeastern corner of the Blackstone neighborhood, near the Seekonk River. The house was a beautiful old brick colonial located on Irving Avenue. From the looks of the exterior, Jolene thought it must have had at least four or five bedrooms on the second floor. Mr. Wharton worked for Terracom Inc. as a regional director for the brand cluster overseeing all their Target, Best Buy, RadioShack, Macy's, and Kmart locations in the area.

Jolene had gone straight to the house from the train station, getting a sense of where it was, before she devised a plan for making contact with Felicia. It was overwhelming. Though she was happy her daughter had stumbled into such a privileged life, she couldn't help but find it unfair. This family could afford, at the very least, to offset enough of the cost of education to secure a tier one sponsorship without having to make any lifestyle changes. They didn't need to adopt a child with a full education voucher.

She found a hostel on the western fringe of downtown Providence and reserved a room with a single bed for a week. It would take a few hours to walk over to the Wharton's neighborhood with the cane and prosthetic, but it was the only place she could afford to stay so many days in a row. For dinner, she ate the last half-piece of Boston cream pie she'd saved from the diner, sipping coffee out of a thermos she'd borrowed from Tammy.

Jolene wanted to go straight back to the Wharton's home, ring the doorbell, and ask to see her daughter. But she restrained herself, not knowing how Felicia might react to the sudden reunion. It had been ten years, which was most of her daughter's childhood. Jolene didn't doubt Felicia would remember her; age five isn't too young for lasting memories and they'd been so close, even for a mother and daughter. But she didn't know the person Felicia had become. Would she be glad to see her mother? Or confused? Or conflicted? Had she suppressed her memories because they were too painful? Could opening old wounds too quickly create new trauma? Was she happy?

She decided to observe Felicia from a distance for a few days

before contacting her, to get a sense of what she was like as a teenager and, hopefully, better understand how to approach her. The
next morning, she went to the Goodwill and picked up a pair
of sunglasses and a wide-brimmed hat to look less recognizable.
Jolene slowly made her way over to the Wharton's neighborhood.
She wasn't sure they'd be home, but it was Sunday so there was no
school. Irving Avenue ran along Blackstone Park, which allowed
her to sit on a bench with a partial view of their house. Since it was
a public park, she wouldn't look suspicious. Two cars were in the
driveway, but there was no activity indicating whether they were
home. She was uneasy thinking about what might happen when she
revealed herself to Felicia and tried to take her mind off it by con-
tinuing her revision of the adventure novel. She put a line through
a sentence: "Stroker was caught between two primal instincts, at
once threatened by the fierce grip the copper-skinned tribeswoman
held on the handle of the macuahuitl while also aroused by the
faint imprint of an aureole pushing against the deerskin blouse
every time she took in a breath." Jolene considered the passage and
then wrote down a revision in the margin: "Stroker was intimidated
by the woman, not so much by her comfort with the large melee
weapon she held in one hand, but by the way the other villagers all
seemed to defer to her judgement."

Two hours later, a woman roughly Jolene's age left the house
with an adolescent boy and a teenage girl. Jolene began to cry
when she got a clear view of the girl's face. She'd grown so much
and looked older than fifteen, but it was Felicia. She laughed at
something the boy said as they all got into one of the cars, a boxy
station wagon shaped like the future trying to look like the past.
They drove away and Jolene paid no attention to which direction
they went. For the next hour and a half, she sat on a bench, smiling

and unaware of anything going on around her. She kept replaying in her head the image of the fifteen-year-old Felicia laughing as she got into the front passenger seat of the car. It was the laugh of a girl who was happy. She was a teenager and there were probably conflicts and heartbreaks in her life, but Felicia didn't carry herself in those few moments like someone who wished to run away from the world she was a part of.

Jolene continued shadowing Felicia and the Whartons for three more days before attempting contact. They appeared to be a relatively normal and content family. Mr. Wharton worked long hours, but when he was present, he was attentive and warm. Jolene assumed Mrs. Wharton had a job as well; she left in the morning with the children and didn't return to the house until she brought them back from school. Sometimes Felicia bickered with her stepbrother and adoptive parents, usually over not being allowed to do something Jolene wouldn't have allowed her to do either. There were limits to these observations. Without a vehicle and still adjusting to moving around with a cane and only one good foot, Jolene's investigation was mostly confined to whatever went on in front of the house, right outside Felicia's school, and the Port City Cafe across the street from the school where Felicia and her friends went for a snack when they had a break during the day or just after the last class.

Jolene wanted so badly to see the way they were inside of their house when nobody outside the family was around. What did they hide from the rest of the world and how did it impact Felicia? Were there abuses that never left the house? Was it all an act, the laughter and warmth? Did Felicia need to be saved? Was she happy?

On her fifth night in Providence, Jolene spent more than usual for dinner and treated herself to her favorite food: a cheeseburger and French fries. She savored every bite as if it were the last meal she'd ever enjoy. It's not as though she were contemplating suicide, but if things didn't go well with Felicia the next day, she wasn't so sure pleasures like taste or smell would mean as much to her anymore. So, she spent the meal thinking about positive outcomes as she slowly consumed the half-pound patty and all its fixings. She wondered if she'd ever eaten beef from a cow with a brain, one that grazed in a field and walked around on four hooves, or if she'd only ever had meat grown in an agrilab. Whatever it had been, it was delicious with Russian dressing and melted cheese. She had a scoop of mint chocolate chip ice cream with hot fudge sauce drizzled over the top for dessert.

For breakfast the next morning, she had a cup of coffee and two packets of oyster crackers she'd swiped from the restaurant the night before. Use of the shower at the hostel cost a dollar a day, so Jolene hadn't bathed since she got to Providence to save some money, but she wanted to look her best for Felicia. After she finished her coffee, she paid the caretaker a dollar and took a ten-minute shower, scrubbing off every little bit of dirt and grime. She used more shampoo than usual because it had a floral scent that could double as a faint perfume.

She put on a pair of pants a little too long for her legs to better disguise her prosthetic foot. There'd be no hiding the awkwardness of her walk, but she wanted to diminish any potential trigger for guilt. She didn't want Felicia to feel bad during their first interaction in a decade. Before Jolene left her room at the hostel, she practiced walking back and forth in movements downplaying her dependency on the cane. She looked herself over once more in the mirror on the back of the door. She hadn't studied her appearance much since her release from prison and took a moment to contemplate how her looks had changed. There was a little weight gain, maybe five pounds or so. She held her posture differently and could see it in her reflection, even when she was standing still.

Jolene decided not to approach Felicia at home. It would likely be construed as an invasion of privacy and not only her daughter's, but of the entire Wharton family. They didn't need to know she'd been watching the house. A public space would be a more appropriate arena for first contact.

Felicia and two of her friends went to the Port City Cafe after school at 3pm. Mrs. Wharton usually picked her up at 3:45pm, which gave Jolene a small window to engage her daughter alone, while Felicia walked from the cafe to the school parking lot where Mrs. Wharton would be waiting for her. Jolene studied her reflection in the passenger side window of a parked car, moving her bangs behind her ears to show more of her face, and then sat down on a public bench outside the cafe. She took out her mechanical pencil to work on the novel, but her hands were shaking too much to write legibly. She tried to focus on her breathing the way Sally B had taught her in prison, to help her shut out the world after her foot had been amputated. It never worked. But trying to make it work had always been better than staring at her bandaged ankle.

When Felicia left the cafe, her stride was confident. She didn't notice anyone around her. She was lost in the screen of her phone, sending messages to the friends she'd just left. Jolene stood up as her daughter walked by laughing at something she was reading.

"Felicia," Jolene said, gently but loud enough to be heard.

Felicia stopped, turned back to the cafe to see if it was one of her friends and then looked around. The moment she locked eyes with her mother, her shoulders dropped down. She nearly fell to the ground. Jolene stepped closer.

"Who are you?" Felicia asked. They both knew that she already knew the answer.

"Felicia, it's me," Jolene responded, moving one step closer. Felicia took two steps back and raised her palm to stop her mother from coming any closer. They let each other absorb the moment before either of them said another word. Felicia's eyes paused on the cane, having noticed the awkwardness of Jolene's movement.

"What are you doing here?" Felicia asked.

"I wanted to see you," Jolene said. "And explain what happened."

"I know where you've been," Felicia said. Her tone was sharp and unkind.

"I'm so sorry," Jolene said, wanting to move closer but respecting her daughter's reluctance.

"What are you doing here?" Felicia asked, again.

"I'm your mother," Jolene said. Not in defiance, but because it was all she could think to say.

"You *were* my mother," Felicia said and began walking away. Jolene followed and, to her surprise, didn't fall too far behind. Felicia was too disoriented to realize how slow she was moving.

Jolene could see Mrs. Wharton up ahead walking towards them. She wanted Felicia's ear for one moment longer before she was swept away by her adoptive mother. She took a receipt out of her pocket and began to write on it.

"Felicia!" She yelled out, desperately. "Stop."

Felicia stopped and turned to Jolene. "What?" she snapped.

Jolene caught up and put the receipt in Felicia's hand. "I'm staying at this hostel downtown. I'll be there for two more nights. Please come visit me. I just want to talk to you, not take you away. If I don't see you by then, I'll leave town."

Mrs. Wharton had reached them and immediately put her arm around Felicia's shoulder.

"Stay away from me!" Felicia shouted, throwing the receipt on the ground. "You're disgusting."

"Felicia!" Mrs. Wharton said as if to softly scold her, but Felicia had started walking towards the car. Mrs. Wharton picked up the receipt and scrutinized Jolene to make sense of the situation, then followed quickly after Felicia.

Jolene made her way back to the bench and collapsed onto the seat and cried for about twenty-five minutes until a policeman came along and told her she was disturbing the customers sitting at tables in front of the cafe. She almost protested because the bench was twenty feet away from the tables and she had the right to sit there, but decided it was pointless to bother and headed back towards the hostel.

On her way back, she went down a side street because it was empty—not a single person in sight. No one to tell her to move along or to stop. No flirts or insults. Just Jolene and the architecture. There was a shuttle stop with a bench halfway down the street where she could sit to rest her legs. She sat down and looked to both ends of the street, but it was still deserted.

There was a small digital advertising screen installed in the interior wall of the shuttle stop. The advertisement on display was for The Touch Corporation. The ad depicted a young woman in lingerie, kneeling on top of a large bed, holding a feather and touching its tip to her bottom lip. The banner text across the top of the screen read: "Where are you ticklish?" Along the bottom of the screen, it read: "Let's find out! The Touch Corporation: For a safe and clean experience, look no further."

Jolene picked up her cane and hit the screen with it as hard as she could, but it was unaffected. She stood up, holding the cane with both hands, and beat the screen repeatedly. The Plexiglas cover was too strong and pliable to be broken by the cane. Then, the Touch Corporation ad was replaced by an ad for a new dairy-free sweet milk drink, which came in five flavors. Jolene lost her desire to smash the screen once it was populated by children sipping on drink boxes and laughing. She turned away and continued her hike back to the hostel.

Later, after a dinner of oyster crackers, Jolene lay on the bed in her room at the hostel, still wearing the same clothes. She'd cried when she first got back to the room, but that had petered out and she was concentrating on the textures and cracks in the paint on the ceiling.

There was a knock on the door. Jolene jumped up in the bed, wanting it to be Felicia knocking, but knowing it wasn't. She walked across the room and opened the door. It was Mrs. Wharton holding the receipt with the address of the hostel written on it. She was alone.

Her hair was brown and styled in a pixie cut. Her clothes were expensive, but not formal. She wore dress sneakers instead of shoes—turquoise and silver jewelry instead of gold and pearls.

Jolene invited her into the room and offered the only chair, but Mrs. Wharton didn't want to sit down.

"I won't be staying long," she said, nervously looking around, uncomfortable with the surroundings.

"How can I help you?" Jolene asked, confident Mrs. Wharton had come to tell her to go away and never bother their family again. She was expecting threats.

"I don't like you," Mrs. Wharton said with a directness Jolene appreciated. "But I also don't like the way Felicia talked to you and then about you after we left. She said horrible things. Things I don't want to repeat. Things I don't want her to say about anyone, ever."

Jolene didn't respond. She didn't know how to. She still wasn't sure why Mrs. Wharton had come to see her. The mood was a mix of apology and antagonism. She remained silent to let it unfold.

Mrs. Wharton looked at the cane and then to Jolene's left foot. "That's how you paid for the education voucher, isn't it? You let them take your foot."

"Yes," Jolene said in a tone declaring her pride as a mother.

"We probably wouldn't have adopted her if she didn't have the voucher," Mrs. Wharton said it as if she were alone and thinking out loud. "We might have, but it was definitely a strong incentive."

"She seems happy," Jolene said, wanting to say something, but still unsure what Mrs. Wharton wanted her to say.

Mrs. Wharton hadn't taken her eyes off the prosthetic.

"Well, you probably know where we live," Mrs. Wharton said. "Felicia and I will be at the picnic tables in the park across the street at 1pm tomorrow. You can join us for lunch if you like. And if she never wants to see you again after that, I want you to leave her alone."

"Thank you," Jolene said.

"This stays between the three of us," Mrs. Wharton said firmly as she walked across the room and opened the door. "If my husband or son find out about this, I'll call the police and tell them you're stalking our family."

"I understand," Jolene said.

"I really do wish you'd never found us," Mrs. Wharton said, looking at Jolene one last time and closing the door behind her.

After a while, Jolene went to see the caretaker and reserved the room for two additional days. She went back upstairs and counted

what remained of her money. She would have to find work soon.
There was more than enough left to pay for the two extra days at
the hostel and the food she'd need to subsist on. She set aside cash
for another outfit from the Goodwill and three more days' worth
of showers.

Jolene couldn't sleep. There was no room for mistakes.

She wanted to bring a gift and tried to remember what Felicia
liked most as a child, focusing on general preferences like colors and
flavors. Blue and vanilla. Magenta and caramel. Orange and mint.
The favorite things a fifteen-year-old would enjoy as much as a five-
year-old. Something that could have endured.

Jolene had already claimed a picnic table. She wanted to be seated
when they arrived to avoid the embarrassment of falling in front of
them. She wore a blue daisy print blouse and black jeans.

Felicia and Mrs. Wharton sat down facing Jolene. Felicia
avoided eye contact. She traced her finger along the edge of one of
the table planks.

"Felicia," Mrs. Wharton said.

"I'm sorry I was so rude to you yesterday," Felica said, insin-
cerely, still looking down.

"That's okay," Jolene responded. "You don't have to apologize.
It was a lot to absorb, and I could have been more sensitive to how
you might react."

Felica looked to Mrs. Wharton, staring her adoptive mother
down as if she were waiting for cues.

"Are chicken sandwiches okay with you for lunch?" Mr. Wharton asked Jolene.

"Oh yes," Jolene answered. "That sounds lovely."

Mrs. Wharton began unpacking the picnic basket as they sat in silence.

"I bought this blouse because it reminded me of how much you loved picking wildflowers when you were little," Jolene said. "Do you still like flowers?"

"Yep," Felicia said. "I still like flowers."

They fell back into silence. Mrs. Wharton handed them plates and napkins, and then served the sandwiches with potato chips and sparkling water.

"And trees," Felicia said. "They're pretty great too."

Jolene smiled to acknowledge the joke. She took a bite of her sandwich, then took another before she'd finished chewing the first. She was starving, but made sure to swallow her mouthful before speaking.

"I've missed you," Jolene said.

Felicia took one small bite of her sandwich and set it back down on the plate. She chewed slowly and swallowed before she looked back across the table.

"You've got two hands," Felicia said. "You could've written a letter or sent an email."

"*Felicia*," Mrs. Wharton snapped. "Don't be unkind. Besides, she wasn't permitted to contact you. Those were the terms. She wasn't even told where you lived."

Felicia's demeanor shifted. She looked a bit surprised, shaken. They all continued to eat their sandwiches for a few minutes. The crunching of potato chips intermittently broke the silence.

"What's that?" Felicia asked, pointing at the small gift Jolene brought.

"It's not much," Jolene said, pushing the gift-wrapped box toward her daughter.

Felica untied the bow and carefully removed the wrapping paper. It was a box of caramels coated with dark chocolate and sea salt.

"You used to love caramel and chocolate together," Jolene said. "The man at the store said the ones with sea salt were the most popular. It's small and if you don't like them, I can take them back."

"This is from Portside Candies," Felicia said.

Jolene nodded.

"These are my favorites," Felicia said.

"It's true. We get her a box every few months," Mrs. Wharton said. "As a special treat."

Jolene smiled.

"Thank you," Felicia said.

She opened the box and ate a caramel, then offered them to her mothers.

Jolene bit into one, closing her eyes as she savored the taste. "They're delicious."

"Does it hurt?" Felicia asked, gesturing to Jolene's feet.

"It was a long time ago," Jolene answered.

"How did it happen?" Felicia asked.

"Machinery," Jolene said. "A freak accident. It was nobody's fault."

Felicia concentrated on the prosthesis. It was fully covered by a sock and pants leg, but she looked upon it as if she had x-ray vision, her mind's eye a microscope. After a minute, she grabbed four caramels and stuffed them all into her mouth.

THE LODGING
OF TIGERS

MARLA STARED DOWN at the half-dried bloodstains on her pants, letting the phone continue to vibrate in her hand. It was Jonathan again. She'd hoped her trip would facilitate a cleaner end, but it hadn't even been a week and he'd already called five times. She'd just left Eddie in critical condition at a hospital in Mae Sot and was sitting in the passenger seat of a jeep, driving off to a small village she'd never heard of before.

They'd startled a wild boar while they were investigating a patch of forest where a tiger had supposedly been spotted. The boar gored Eddie's thigh, fracturing his femur in a few places and taking out a hunk of flesh the size of a toddler's fist. They were isolated from the rest of the expedition party when it happened. Marla's tranquilizer gun jammed, so she had to drop it and take up Eddie's rifle to protect them. The boar was still attacking Eddie, pushing him against a tree trunk, its tusk caught between his bone and the surrounding flesh. She shot the boar through the neck, wounding it enough that it fell to the ground, but then she had to listen to it squealing while she put pressure on Eddie's wound to stop the bleeding. It took fifteen minutes for the group to find them, and when they did Marla shouted "kill it" repeatedly until one of their guides executed the pig with a bullet through its head.

She didn't want to leave Eddie in the hospital room alone.

He was unconscious and Marla wanted to be there when he woke up, but she'd received word two local hunters had captured a male Indochinese tiger in the wild. They were willing to sell it to her, but she only had two hours to barter the deal. After that, they'd seek out buyers on the black market, which meant the animal would probably be slaughtered and sold in pieces. It was maybe the last of its subspecies. She reminded herself there's no adapting to extinction.

But, as the jeep barreled further away from the hospital, she couldn't help thinking about how Eddie's Thai was even worse than hers and how much more confusing that would make it for him when he woke up alone. She tapped *ignore* on her phone, wondering when Jonathan would take the hint. With Eddie out of commission, she had to settle for their conservation intern Larry as her wingman, which wasn't the worst-case scenario. She found him slightly obnoxious, but manageable. There was never any weird energy between them and the only desire he'd ever exhibited in front of her was for evaluation and recognition. He was a good scientific researcher for his age, but nervous in the field. As long as she told him he was doing a good job, everything should be fine. The screen on her phone lit up, indicating a voice message from Jonathan.

She'd decided to end the relationship two weeks earlier as they laid in bed one night after sex and he waxed poetic about how much he loved her "deep espresso skin" while he caressed her with two fingers. But the truth was, she'd been bored with him for quite some time and his tender racism only sped up the inevitable conclusion. The problem with Jonathan was he didn't offset the imbalance. In the beginning, he was interesting. Good-looking and accomplished and tall, he was a professor of anthropology who'd been tenured at the age of twenty-nine. He spoke four languages fluently and had traveled to over fifty countries, immersing himself in culture after culture. He'd already published three books by the time she'd met him when he was thirty-eight. Yet, despite his many bells and whistles, she found him incredibly dull after her initial excitement wore off. He was the kind of person who needed to be sitting at a table surrounded by books to come up with something sharp and interesting to say; he could never improvise his wit.

The jeep reached the address given to them for the rendezvous. The small building looked like a bar that was closed. A Chang beer sign hung in the window in front of a red curtain. The driver was the same guide who killed the boar. His name was Somsak and he was the only local Marla felt she could mostly trust. She didn't trust anyone completely, but Somsak's behavior hadn't suggested any troubling motivations as far as she could tell. He did the job he was paid for; his actions were all very cause and effect. He was the one who killed the boar because he wasn't apprehensive. It had to be done and he did it. There was no pause and he didn't dwell on what he'd done. He put the animal out of its misery, field-dressed it, and took the carcass for meat. She felt safer with him.

The translator Marla and her team had been using was waiting outside for them. He went by the name Reggie and wore a New York Yankees cap. He had set up the meeting with the hunters and would act as translator for the negotiations to purchase the tiger. Marla was suspicious Reggie was an associate of the hunters and that his role as objective mediator was not without its loyalties—a hunch only reinforced by the look of distrust on Somsak's face every time Reggie spoke.

"Marla, you are beautiful as always," Reggie said with palms out as if to hug without touching. "How is Eddie?"

"I don't know," she said, not wanting to think about it until she was back at the hospital. "Where are the sellers?"

"They are waiting for us inside," he said. "We must not delay; they have already received two other offers."

"Show us the way," Marla said. She saw Somsak tuck his pistol into the waist of his pants at the small of the back and cover it up with the tail of his shirt. Larry was uneasy and fixated on the weapon.

"Larry," she said quietly, redirecting his attention. "We have nothing to worry about. He's just cautious, which is a good thing."

Marla didn't entirely believe her own words, but if Larry fell apart, the likelihood of a seamless negotiation decreased significantly.

"I don't feel good," Larry said, pulling at the outer tip of an eyebrow with a thumb and index finger.

"Pull it together," she said, gently gripping his wrist to guide the arm down to his side.

Reggie opened the door and held it, gesturing for Marla to go first. There were seven tables inside the bar and only one of them had its chairs down. It was in the middle of the room and two men were sitting, facing the door. Four other men were standing, all of them armed. Three open seats were waiting for Marla, Larry, and Reggie. The rest of the building appeared empty, no bartender or tiger in sight. On top of the table was a bottle of Thai rum in a bucket of ice and five short glasses with melting ice cubes.

They all sat down at the table except for Somsak, who stood behind them, near the door. One of the two seated hunters picked up the bottle and filled all the glasses halfway with rum. He raised his glass and waited for everybody else to raise theirs, then said, "Cheers." Everyone with a glass repeated the word and took a sip. This was followed by a short silence, both sides of the table waiting for the other to begin the negotiations.

"Where's the tiger?" Marla asked. Reggie spoke with the men in Thai.

"The tiger is at a different location," Reggie said. "Catching and selling tigers is a crime that carries a severe penalty, no matter who is buying. They wanted to meet you first and make sure it is not a trap by the government."

"When can we see the tiger?" she asked. Reggie conferred with the men.

"They want one million US dollars," Reggie said. "For the last Indochinese tiger, they feel it is a fair price."

"That's a lot of money," Marla said, "and I'm not going to start negotiating a price until I see the animal and examine it."

Reggie relayed her message. The two seated hunters spoke amongst themselves, and then responded looking at Marla instead of Reggie.

"They need to make a phone call to arrange a visit to go see the tiger and they ask you to wait here for a few minutes," Reggie said. The two men got up and left with Reggie through the doorway behind them. Two of the standing men followed and two stayed behind.

The room was quiet. Marla could tell Larry wanted to speak by the way his lips teased the beginnings of syllables. But he kept his relative cool and didn't utter a word.

Marla decided to listen to Jonathan's voice messages while she waited. He'd left five and she never erased messages before listening to them, even if she knew she didn't want to hear anything the person had to say and had no intention of responding. It was a violation of good manners in her mind. She could pass by someone she knew on the street and ignore them, pretending she didn't see them without thinking twice about it. But voicemail was a social contract she felt obligated to honor. She played the first message, from three days earlier: *Marla, I know you're halfway across the world right now and this isn't the right time to have a talk about us. But, can we meet when you return? I just don't think we should be hasty. Safe Journeys.* Marla erased the message and played the next, left one day later: *Hi. If you're listening to this, then you also heard my last message. I don't expect you to call back, especially while you're away. Really. I don't. But if you could send an email or text message and let me know whether you're willing to open up a dialogue between us or if I should just move on. I don't want to do that, and I don't think you want to either. I miss you. Not because I'm lonely and need to be with someone, but because I want to be with you.* She erased the message and that it was only the second out of five brought about a sense of dread. She looked around the room. Larry was reading email on his phone, trying his best to appear calm. Somsak and the other two men were standing still like statues of soldiers at a war memorial, stoic and cold. Marla finished what remained in her glass. One of the standing men immediately walked over, added four ice cubes to her empty glass, and filled it three quarters of the way with rum. She played the next message, left four hours after the last: *I'm not asking for much, only a few words. Some indication as to where we really stand. I deflected a lovely young historian who flirted with me at a gallery opening this evening. Good night.* Six hours later, he left the next message: *Well, good morning. I'm feeling down; it hurts that you're not responding at all. I just want to try to make things work. Maybe they won't. Maybe this is futile. A waste of my time, which is valuable. I have a lot going on in my life. But I really want to try. I don't know what else there is to say.* Reggie and the other four men re-entered the room before she could listen to the final message.

Reggie walked over and sat back down at the table, but the rest of the men remained standing. Marla put down her phone, annoyed by Jonathan's messages and took another big sip of rum to ease her nerves.

"We can go visit the tiger now," Reggie said, wearing a salesman's smile. "But there are conditions. You must wear blindfolds and hoods during the drive. And you will leave your phones here so they may not be used for tracking. And, also, only you and Larry are permitted to go. Somsak must stay. You understand?"

Marla touched her palm softly to Larry's shoulder to stop him from protesting

"That's fine," she responded to Reggie. "But this will only be to examine the tiger. There will be no transaction until we return and make the exchange at a neutral location—that is, if we decide to purchase the animal. You understand?"

Reggie turned back to the men and spoke in Thai. They didn't say anything, but the man who appeared to be senior in both age and body language nodded to Reggie in response.

"That is acceptable, Marla," Reggie said.

They all stood up. Larry looked at Marla and didn't have to say anything to communicate his fear. She put out her hand to collect his cellphone. He did nothing.

"It will be okay," Marla whispered. "I need you with me and I need you to keep it together."

Larry handed his phone to her and then she handed both of their phones to Somsak, who looked her in the eyes and shook his head slowly.

"Hold on to these for us," she said.

Somsak took the phones and whispered, "Want a gun?"

"No," Marla said. "But thank you."

Marla and Larry followed Reggie and all but two of the men

out the back door. They were taken to two jeeps parked in the dirt lot behind the building. Once they were seated inside one of the jeeps, Reggie handed each of them a black cloth. After the blindfolds were tied tightly and black hoods were also pulled over their heads, the vehicles started moving. The ride only lasted for about thirty minutes, but due to the bumpiness of the roads, Marla found it difficult to calculate how many times they'd turned. So, she had no idea how far they'd travelled. They could have been going in circles the whole time. They could be five blocks from where they started or ten miles for all she knew. When Reggie told them to take the blindfolds off, they were parked inside a large warehouse-sized garage without windows, the kind that could house large semi-trailers. Outside of their immediate parking area, the interior of the structure had been partitioned with several makeshift walls separated by narrow hallways.

The partition walls only went up about eight feet, not even reaching halfway to the ceiling. They were too tall for Marla to see what was contained within them, but the sounds were unsettling. The whole space reverberated with a chorus of suffering. Some tones sounded muffled by total enclosure while others echoed in the open air. She couldn't tell how many animals or how many different species were being held captive inside the building because there were so many whimpers and cries that they all muddled together. She could tell there were birds and mammals, predators and prey, but it was as if they'd all melted into one agonizing plea. It was the worst thing she'd ever heard. When she turned back to look at Larry, he silently mouthed, "What the fuck?"

At least another dozen armed men were visible when they got out of the jeeps and there was no way of knowing how many more were scattered throughout the building or keeping guard just outside.

"Don't ask any questions about this place," Marla whispered in Larry's ear. "We're only here to see and talk about the tiger."

Four men stepped forward; one of them spoke to Reggie, who then looked back to Marla and Larry, gesturing for them to follow. They walked down one of the hallways, men in front of and behind them. Marla counted eight doors on each side of the hallway and behind each door were cries and moans. There was nothing defiant in the sounds emanating from these rooms. None of the animals Marla heard sounded as if they'd been recently placed into captivity, but instead broken down from weeks or months of confinement. Beasts who'd surrendered their fight.

Six doors down on the right, the group halted. Part of Marla wanted to turn and run back to the jeep, not wanting to see what shadow of a tiger remained. But, when the door was opened for her, she walked towards it. The smell hit her before she could see into the room, a powerful odor of excrement and sweat wafted out. The room was small, perhaps ten feet by seven feet, and the back half was a cage. The remnants of an apex predator lay inside, pushing itself up to all fours with great difficulty when she entered. She could hear Larry gasp a little behind her. It let out a low whimpering growl and was so emaciated the shape of its rib cage could be seen under its coat every time it took in a slow breath. Marla noticed both upper canines had been removed when the tiger opened its mouth. She wanted to open the cage and unleash the animal on its captors, watch it tear down several men and have its fill of their warm flesh before it was struck down in a blaze of glory. She took a moment and let the daydream play out in her head.

It was a male Indochinese specimen as promised, but it had been some time since he roamed freely, if he ever had. Watching the tiger struggling to stand up offered Marla no evidence the subspecies still existed in the wild, and she was suspecting more and more the alleged sightings were false rumors spread by this group of poachers to put a high price tag on a broken animal. The whole trip was shaping up to be a con. If Reggie was in on it, they knew she was fully funded by Phyla Technologies, which meant they also knew the animal's DNA was worth a fortune to her benefactor—the company didn't need a healthy beast to make one. The sellers would have reached out to her because she was even further removed from the government than the company; if the government found out, they'd arrest the poachers, confiscate the tiger, and then sell it to Phyla at a markup. But the company preferred dealing with the poachers directly.

Larry was pale as bone. Marla was starting to feel sick. She wanted to undo the poachers' operation but had no idea where they were and that's why they didn't allow Somsak to accompany them. He probably could have roughly pieced it together, even with a blindfold around his eyes and hood pulled down over his head. Her only option was to save the tiger, not the menagerie.

"I'll give you eight hundred thousand US dollars for the tiger," Marla said, trying to sound inflexible. It was a lot of money for such a sick animal, but it was Phyla's money and the animal would be better off with her at the conservancy. Reggie relayed her offer and one of the men responded.

"The price was one million," Reggie said.

"That was for a wild tiger," she argued. "This animal has been in a cage for a long time. I should cut the price in half. Eight hundred thousand is a lot more than they'll get on the black market."

Reggie translated what she said and there was a brief conversation between three of the older men. One of the men stepped forward and put out his hand to Marla and they shook on it.

"It is a deal," Reggie said. "Now we can return to the bar and work out the details of the exchange."

When they got back to the bar and took the blindfolds off, Marla was relieved to be in Somsak's presence again. She immediately felt safer as he returned their phones. She made a call to the acquisitions department at Phyla to discuss the purchase. Once she confirmed the animal as an Indochinese tiger, the request for funds was approved and she was transferred to the shipping and transportation department to arrange the tiger's delivery to the United States. The Thai government wouldn't interfere with the transport after the transaction was complete because they wouldn't want to jeopardize their own fruitful relationship with Phyla.

Marla was sitting at the table in the bar. The ice had long melted, so she poured herself a shot of rum, neat. Larry sat down next to her. He'd gone to the bathroom fifteen minutes earlier to vomit. Marla poured another shot of rum and pushed it towards him. He drank his rum and then poured some water from the ice bucket into his glass. When he finished the water, Marla poured him another shot.

"He'll be better off with us," she said.

"I know," Larry responded.

"He might actually be the last Indochinese tiger born in the wild," she said. "That's something."

"It is," he said.

They both emptied their glasses and poured another round, gesturing for Somsak to join them, but he declined. When they were done drinking, Somsak drove them back to the hospital to check in on Eddie. Reggie accompanied them as translator. Eddie was asleep, but they talked to the doctor. He'd been able to stop the bleeding, but the wound was infected, and the femur bone was crushed badly in three places. If there was no infection, then maybe the bones could slowly heal, but amputation was their only option under the circumstances. The doctor told them Eddie needed to be prepped for surgery and they wouldn't be able to see him before-hand, but he could have visitors the next day between noon and three p.m.

Somsak drove Marla and Larry back to their hotel from the hospital. It was early evening. Marla stayed in the front passenger seat of the jeep after Larry got out.

"I was glad to have you on our team," she said to Somsak, not knowing what else to say.

"You are welcome," Somsak responded, which led to a moment of silence, awkward but not uncomfortable. "The tiger will be safe with you. It will be a better home."

"Do you have a family?" She asked.

"Yes," he said. "A wife and son and two daughters."

Marla stared through the windshield for a moment and then unclasped the necklace she was wearing, hidden under her shirt. It was an antique made of emeralds and gold, the only gift from Jona-than she'd planned on keeping. She placed it in Somsak's hands and told him it was for his wife.

"No," Somsak said. "I cannot."

"Please," she said, leaving the gift with him and getting out of the jeep. Marla leaned in and gave Somsak a warm smile. "Thank you."

Somsak stopped trying to hand the necklace back and nodded his head to her. "Good luck."

Marla closed the door to the jeep and went up to her hotel room. When she looked at her phone for the first time in an hour, she saw there was a new message from Jonathan. She listened to the message she hadn't heard earlier: *I saw that young historian again last night at a talk given by a visiting professor on the use of quipu in the Inca civilization. We went out for drinks after. Then we went back to her apartment and made love. Twice. She appreciates me and what I have to offer. I've decided that I can no longer allow myself to be taken for granted. Goodbye.* Marla deleted the message and listened to the most recent, left while she visited the tiger: *If I don't hear from you in the next twenty-four hours, I don't ever want you to contact me again.* She put her phone on the nightstand and laid down in bed, closing her eyes and thinking about Eddie's leg. Her thoughts drifted to the tiger's missing teeth, wondering what ailment they'd been used as treatment for. Perhaps they were bought as a powder by some desperate parents hoping it would cure their child's rabies.

Four days later, Marla sat in the hospital room where Eddie was recovering. He'd just woken up and it was the first time she'd seen him since the amputation that he wasn't delirious from morphine and whatever else they'd given him to help manage the pain. Twice the day before, he talked to her as if they were sitting in the jeep on their way to the forest where he was attacked by the boar like he was stuck in a time warp. But he was back to being the Eddie she knew and fully aware of what had happened to him.

"Did you find the tiger?" Eddie asked.

"Yeah," Marla answered. "We did."

"And we're taking it back to the States with us?" He asked, hopeful.

"We are," she said.

"What condition was it in?" He asked.

"He was in bad shape," Marla said. "He'd been mistreated and malnourished for a long time."

They were quiet for at least a minute, which was unusual. They were usually chatty with each other. It was their way. Eddie looked down towards his lap.

"It was a strong leg," Eddie said.

Marla looked at his upper thigh near the hip, where the leg now ended, then let her eyes follow the absence down to where his foot would have been. She remembered fondly the few times they'd slept together and how much she'd enjoyed gripping his legs like handrails when she was on top of him.

"It was indeed," she said, smiling at him.

She thought about the tiger. It was already being transported back to the States. She hoped it would survive the journey, though she didn't anticipate a long and happy life. Due to its deteriorating condition, Phyla would immediately extract and preserve every piece of usable biology they could from the animal. It would not likely survive the series of procedures involved.

But the conservancy had been promised four healthy cloned Indochinese tigers in addition to the fee for their services plus expenses. The tiger would live on, she told herself, and with no memory of this horrible life.

THE BOOK
PREACHER

HE SEARCHES FOR his next disciple. Broken vessels waiting to be picked up and put on the path to enlightenment.

A woman walks down the street shifting and turning as if she's trying to get away from her own body. Her eyes are filled with something toxic and cheap. Her clothes, hair, and skin are stained with dirt. A very small metal crucifix hangs down from her neck. The Book Preacher notices all of it and approaches her.

His nice suits make him look out of place and eccentric. Not only because they're finer than any of the clothes worn by the types of people in the types of places he frequents, but also because they're fashions from a different time. He even has a pocket watch in a watch pocket with a chain attached to the buttonhole on his vest. The Book Preacher stands in disharmony with the day, but sticks to neighborhoods the city and its councils often neglect and ignore. Districts filled with violence and addiction. Despite their dangers, these neighborhoods provide refuge for those trying to go unnoticed or those who have nobody and nowhere else to turn—bountiful with what the Book Preacher calls easy fruit.

The woman is stumbling a little with each step, but he waits until she trips and nearly falls to the ground before he steps in, catching her arm and shoulder to help lift her back up on two feet. She smiles without eye contact and looks weary. Thank you, she says, and begins to move away. He asks if she's all right. Nothing I can't walk off, she says.

His skin is like fine bronze. His hair is cut short, but curly like the tendrils of a grapevine. He claims to be of mixed heritage. His mother's family, so he tells it, were Blacks from the Delta who spent their lives working hard and fearing the Lord. His father was a minister and founder of a denomination he called Native Christianity, which chose to believe the roots of the divine father began on the American continents with its indigenous peoples. His father's father was a Pentecostal snake-handler and faith healer. His father's mother was a shaman, a pueblo spirit doctor who walked the earth with the ghosts of coyotes and armadillos. But those are all lies. The Book Preacher is actually made up of all-white lapsed Catholic European blood from South Jersey. His complexion is cultivated by his own design. He travels with the seasons, spending spring and summer up North and fall and winter down South, so he can lie in the sun a little every day, year-round. He's not fooling anyone with his complexion, but he's good-looking and tall and intimidating. His strange, old-fashioned charisma confuses people.

"Stop the things you're doing to yourself," he says to the woman.

"What do you know about what I do?" she asks, resentfully, with her back to him.

"Everywhere you go, times are hard," he responds softly. "Harder than they've ever been before."

She turns to face him, letting herself fall against the wall of a building as if she meant to lean. She puts on her best I'm-on-to-you face. She knows that this man is bad news and doesn't trust him, not one bit. His insights are either vague or obvious. But, still, the way he speaks with that warmth and a relaxed openness seems genuine somehow. Maybe because there's no urgency to his approach and it's hard not to enjoy the sound of his voice. It's deep and soft.

The Book Preacher always carries a small Bible with a worn reddish-brown leather cover in one of his hands. He often speaks in passages that are not his own, from the Good Book or song, mostly spirituals and popular blues lyrics.

"These times will make you go from door to door," he says, not moving any closer to the woman. "Begging for each and every meal. It's no way to live."

The Book Preacher grips the lapels of his jacket and pulls them open slightly allowing her to see the cash just barely peeking out from an inside pocket and the full sag of his gold watch chain.

"And what are you going to do about it?" she asks. The woman has a look to her like she's strategizing a Plan B to rob him if he turns out to be false, which he probably is.

The Book Preacher tells the woman there's nothing he can do about it. He can offer himself up as a companion for moral and spiritual support, but she's going to have to pull herself up by her own bootstraps in order to redeem herself in the Lord's eyes.

She asks him if he has a congregation, half-serious. The Book Preacher holds his Bible up in front of her and says he brings his chapel with him wherever he goes, then invites her to a place he knows of nearby where it's private enough to receive her confession. She accepts and follows, believing he's underestimating her more than she's underestimating him. But, she's wrong. They're always wrong, every one of them.

The Book Preacher gently grips her elbow and leads her down the street, reciting verses and looking up at the sky.

You follow them, staying far enough behind that he won't notice. Even if you lose them, you know where he's taking her. You've followed him there before.

———————

You'd been searching for your brother for nearly five months. When things were in a more positive place, you'd talk to each other at least once a week. But, when Peter was going through one of his rougher patches, he'd often fall out of touch and would be hard to locate for extended stretches of time. Never for more than two months, though. This recent silence was the longest it had ever been. You were terrified and couldn't imagine anything besides death could have estranged the two of you for so long.

When Peter finally called, you'd never been so relieved in your entire life. He sounded good, at first. He was enthusiastic and spoke clearly in complete sentences—usually when coming out of a dark period his language was choppy and incoherent. You asked him how he was and where he'd been. He told you he'd been in Newark for a while and had recently moved on to Boston and that's when he started talking about the Book Preacher. Peter didn't go into much detail except that he'd found purpose in his life and felt God was with him. Mostly, he stressed how everything was fine and you should stop looking for him. He planned to return home in another four months for a visit, but until then would be too busy to be in touch on a regular basis. He told you he loved you, adding he believed you could be saved, and then hung up.

As relieved as you'd been to hear from him, this was not the Peter you'd protected and cared for since you were both children. The Peter on the phone was changed. It was not Peter high or sober or happy. He sounded as if he'd been taken and didn't know it. After you'd thought about the conversation for a while, you redialed the number, which came from the common phone at a hostel in Boston. You let your office know you'd have to work remotely for the next week and left in your car to find your brother. Even under the most extreme circumstances, you tried to avoid using up your vacation days. There were so few of them.

When you reached your destination, you immediately started asking about your brother, canvassing the area around the hostel. Nobody positively identified Peter, but when you mentioned the Book Preacher, most people thought they knew who you were talking about. They'd ask if you meant the man in the old fancy suit with the antique watch and you'd say yes even though you had no idea. They told you if you hung around the neighborhood for a few days, he'd probably show up, walking the streets with a tattered Bible, proselytizing to just one person, never a group.

The next day you saw the Book Preacher for the first time. He was approaching a man who was jittery and malnourished. The Book Preacher started talking, eventually gesturing his arm northbound on Washington Street. They walked to one of the more isolated pockets of the neighborhood and entered a shanty up against the back of an old apartment building. You moved in close and looked through the window, which was cracked open. The interior was simple but lived in—a cot, a table with two chairs, a suitcase, six nice suits hanging from a pole, a bottle of whiskey, a single lamp plugged into a small generator, and a couple of old wooden cigar boxes side-by-side on the counter next to bottle of red wine and a small gold-plated chalice. They both sat down at the table and the Book Preacher handed the man a piece of bread broken off from a loaf. He spoke of God and how we can all do our part to contribute to mankind's salvation.

The Book Preacher stood up and walked over to the counter, asking the man if he'd take the body and blood of Christ as he poured some wine into the chalice and opened both cigar boxes. The man said yes, he would. The Book Preacher laid a handkerchief over his right shoulder, and then took two pieces of communion wafer, each from different cigar boxes, holding them in separate hands, picked up the chalice, and returned to the table. After blessing the body and blood, he ate his wafer and drank from the chalice, wiping off the rim with the handkerchief. He offered the other wafer to the man, who ate it and then drank from the chalice.

The Book Preacher held his small red leather Bible in his left palm and asked the man to place his hand on top of it. As he began to talk about salvation, you watched the Book Preacher make repetitive motions with the pocket watch in his other hand. Your view was slightly obstructed and moving any closer could have exposed you.

Eventually, he asked the man to close his eyes and imagine Paradise. The Book Preacher described dozens upon dozens of plants and animals from all corners of the world living in a vast garden together. A camel thorn tree's longest branch scratched the belly of a baobab mingling amongst firs and hemlocks. Birch trees unraveled from their paper outfits. The aerial roots of a massive banyan arose in front of a sequoia cluster. Japanese maples, beech trees, sugar maples, sassafras, and swamp tupelos offered a patch of constant autumn. A large willow drooped over jade plants and juniper bonsais. Morning glories and trumpet flowers crept purple and orange through shrubs and trunk bottoms. Saguaros and jumping chollas warded off intrusions with their spines. This wall of vegetation went on and on, farther than any mortal eye can see, offering protection to all the garden's beasts. Every species was represented. A pinto raced a chestnut-colored Arabian across the plain, dodging bison, okapi, moose, yak, and kudu. A barn owl landed on the shoulder of a black rhino, causing it to charge into the middle of a gaggle of geese. A lion, awoken by a timber wolf's howl, shook out his mane and roared to drown out all other sounds. A spirit bear peered over, unperturbed, and continued foraging for berries. There was no bloodshed and no hunger either. It reminded you of a television commercial for Phyla you'd seen a few times, but more poetic.

Bordering the garden was a sea of glass, prismatic and forever. It was beautiful. You wanted badly to wade into its depths until you were swallowed whole. Disturbed by the bewitchment, you left and walked back to your room at the Hotel Chanticleer. In its day, the hotel was probably quite nice, but that was some time ago.

This ritual with the wafer, wine, and watch was repeated every afternoon around the same time. There was one day, after the Book Preacher sent the man out to run an errand, you spied on him taking out two amber-colored dropper bottles. He then added a few drops from each to several communion wafers and let them fully absorb before placing them in the same cigar box containing the wafers he always gave to the other man.

Several days later, you were following them to a different neighborhood, not too far away, but outside of the radius of their usual walkabout. The Book Preacher was wearing a black clergy shirt with a Roman collar, a style you'd never seen him in before. They stopped in the middle of a block and the Book Preacher whispered something to the man. The man entered a discount jewelry store with a canvas bag in his hand, and the Book Preacher walked in thirty seconds later. You got close enough that you could look through the window. Instead of security cameras, they had a Rottweiler. Within a few seconds, the man was screaming and swinging the bag around. He smashed the bag through the glass of a display case, and then began smashing the other display cases with his bare hands, eventually grabbing a glass shard and slicing it into his own arm. The dog went after him. While the store employees pulled the dog away and subdued the man, the Book Preacher retrieved the bag, swiping several pieces of jewelry, which he then put in his pocket without anybody noticing. He handed the bag to one of the employees and asked if he could help. They asked if he could give them some space and that the store was closed for business until the police arrived to take the man into custody. The Book Preacher told them he would pray for this troubled soul and left.

After a week and a half following the Book Preacher around, there was no sign of your brother, but you decided to stay around until you found him or at least discovered what happened to him. Not knowing how deeply your brother might be involved in the Book Preacher's business, you didn't want to get the police involved—not until you knew for sure he'd be better off in prison.

One afternoon, the Book Preacher sat next to you at the counter of the neighborhood diner and asked you why you'd been following him around. You were startled, but recovered with the story you'd prepared, telling him you needed guidance to learn how you could best serve the Lord. You were new to the area and someone told you about the Book Preacher. Being naturally shy, you were building up the courage to introduce yourself. He smiled, telling you not to be afraid and that all he ever had in store for anybody was to share God's love with them.

———————————

You never accept the wafer. You tell him you don't need it because you already feel the body and blood coursing through your veins. The Book Preacher smiles at your rejections. When he talks, you only fully listen when the conversation is equally back and forth. Once he begins to ramble on, asking you to imagine a better place, you drown out his words with your own. Sometimes you sing your favorite song to yourself, the one you're too embarrassed of to confess to anyone. Other times you count backwards from a number like nine-hundred-eighty-three because it takes more concentration than counting forwards and starting on a random odd number avoids falling into easy patterns. Then, you stop at another random odd number along the way and break into song. It's different every time. All you have to do is embrace some chaos. He needs every piece of your mind to have you. He needs you to take the wafer and listen for you to be his.

One morning over breakfast at the diner, the Book Preacher tells you he thinks you're not exactly who you say you are. He tells you he knows the difference between someone who wants to run things and someone who wants to serve. You feel his words in your stomach. The Book Preacher notices your anxiety. His eyes follow the subtle shift of your body facing out from the booth, ready to get up and walk out the door, but he makes no motions against your flight. Instead, he leans back in his seat. He's completely relaxed. Your survival instinct tells you to run and keep running. Your brother is lost and he's not coming back.

"Everybody needs somebody," the Book Preacher says, looking for your server and pointing to both coffee cups. He thanks her when she comes over and refills them.

You put yourself in check. You recognize there are three of you, presently, and they're at odds with each other: the you who wants to run, the you who wants to save your brother, and then the one who likes the sound of the book preacher's voice. You remain seated.

"It can be lonely on the road," the Book Preacher confesses to you. "No one to lean on. No one to share in your triumphs."

You begin to wonder how much he knows you know about him

and, of that, how much he's letting on he knows you know. In the end, you decide not to run.

"What do you have in mind?" you say, trying to sound hesitant as if you're willing to hear him out, but not ready to shake hands on it.

He tells you there's no reason to rush into anything. Better to take a few days to make sure your talents complement each other. He invites you to lunch the next day, then pays the tab and leaves. You sit in the booth for another ten minutes alone to collect and calm yourself.

Over the next week, the two of you meet for meals and go for walks around the neighborhood. The conversations are tame. Nothing incriminating is revealed. The Book Preacher is observing you, trying to get a feel for what you're after.

You continue to follow him, putting just a little more distance between the two of you and trying your best to look less conspicuous.

At lunch one day, he shares a plan he has for a congregation down south. A job he's had his eye on for over a year, but way too ambitious a project to take on alone. You'd pose as a preacher and minister who run a Christian-themed tour group selling two separate international trips: one visiting several geographical locations of significance in the Old Testament and the other visiting sites of significance in the New Testament. The plan would be to sell about twenty packages for each trip. For the most part, it'd be a two-person job, but you'd have to hire someone to design a website to pull it off, to make the travel company seem believable. The Book Preacher knows a guy who can make it look sleek and once he's been paid, the rest of the take split down the middle will be enough for each of you to start a nice little nest egg.

The Book Preacher asks you to take the rest of the day to think it over and meet him for coffee the next morning.

You're bothered by how easily the Book Preacher is opening up his world to you and confused about why he's inviting you to join him on the job. It seems out of character with his working patterns. Even though you've only been investigating him a short time, you've never seen him work with a partner. His only associates have been those under his control, which makes you wonder about the woman. You haven't seen her around him for a couple of days.

You reconcile with yourself that if you ever want to see your brother again, you'll have to get close to the Book Preacher. You have coffee with him the next day and tell him you're interested in moving forward on the job he'd proposed. You reserve the right to back out at any time if something doesn't feel right because those are the terms the person you're pretending to be would agree to. He smiles wide and presses his little red Bible against his chest as if his faith means something to him. You wonder if the line between the Book Preacher and the man behind the Book Preacher gets hazy sometimes and if you can use it to your advantage.

The Book Preacher sets up a meeting with the website designer for ten in the evening to discuss the concept for the company and how to implement its online presence.

———————————

You meet him on the corner of Ellery and Washington Street. The Book Preacher says you're going to the web designer's place to see the specs he's already drawn up. You're walking south on Washington and turn right down an alley. The Book Preacher talks more than he ever has before. He's expressive and animated, describing in detail his vision for the website and where he thinks he'll butt heads with the designer, but insists you'll both need to be firm. After all, you're going be the ones who have to sell it.

You've been keeping such a close eye on him that you haven't been paying attention to the surroundings. When he stops and turns around, you notice you're far down an alley off of another alley and can no longer see the street or any other people. You reach your hand into your coat pocket and take hold of your handgun.

"I know who you are," the Book Preacher says. "He told me."

"Who told you what?" you ask, backing up a few paces.

You feel a sharp and deep pain in your lower back, under your ribcage to the right of the spinal column, and then another. You touch your hand to the spot where it hurts and bring it back in front of you to see it's covered in blood.

You turn and face a man, changed and emaciated by the mileage of his addiction and enslavement, but you recognize this man to be your brother.

You start to scream, but he covers your mouth and pushes you up against the wall of the alley. You hope your eyes on his will snap him out of it and he'll immediately rip off his shirt and press it against your wounds to stop the bleeding. He stabs you again and again. You pull his hand away and say please don't, we're family. And he stabs you again. You say please stop, Peter, I love you. He puts his hand back over your mouth and stabs you again.

The Book Preacher says that's enough, we must give her space to repent her sins. Peter says of course, Father, and stops. You fall down. The Book Preacher tells your brother he has proven his devotion to the Lord and can now join the rest of the chosen peoples in the sea of glass. Peter says thank you, oh thank you. The Book Preacher takes out a straight razor and slashes your brother's throat. Peter grabs the wound and collapses. The Book Preacher walks over and squats next to you. He takes out a handkerchief and wipes his prints off the handle of the razor.

"As many as I love, I rebuke and chasten," he says, placing the straight razor in your hand and closing your fingers around the handle.

"Why?" you say.

"Because you're lukewarm, and neither cold nor hot," he says, setting his handkerchief on fire with a lighter and watching it burn to ash. He sits down, cross-legged, as if he were warming himself next to a campfire. He waits to leave until no bloodstained cloth remains.

You try to let go of the razor, but you only have enough strength left to breathe, barely.

"It's not so bad," he says to you as he stands up and your eyes begin to close. "I wouldn't mind dying if dying was all."

PROTECTED
LAND

MY SHARE OF the morsel should have lasted for at least a week or two, keeping me nice and steady—two or three days if I really wanted to get drenched and lose my feet. I needed to float away for a little while before I could even begin to think about what had happened to me and Kelsie. About all those different little bodies and how they worked so well together.

The van that had come for us was matte black. We'd scraped together enough morsel to take the edge off for the job—just a little trickle. Two ski masks were laying on a bench in the back with a note asking we wear them to hide our faces. There were no windows. It made sense they wouldn't want us to find the house again.

The man with the nice sunglasses who'd approached us the day before about robbing his parents for him told us to steal a solid gold egg, about the size of a chicken's, sitting in a wicker nest. It would be on the desk in his father's study on the first floor. He'd told us it really stood out.

The van stopped and we put our masks on before the door opened.

"Mine smells weird," Kelsie said.

"Get over it," I responded.

"It's strong," she said. "Like somebody pissed in it."

"This won't take long."

We got out next to a perimeter brick wall. I couldn't make out any street signs or landmarks or even any other houses—it wasn't a familiar neighborhood. The driver kept his distance and pointed to a door along the wall without grumbling a word.

It was unlocked. Kelsie gestured for me to go first.

When we entered, the trees and bushes were so dense and high up, we couldn't see anything else, but there was a single path leading down what appeared to be the middle of the property. We must have walked for two minutes through the thick and still no sign of a house. It was lush and terrifying like an enchanted forest where my greatest dreams and nightmares lurked around every corner. I could have sworn it moved, reaching in every direction and crying out in hunger as if it was getting dry like me and not because of the wind.

"How big is this place?" Kelsie whispered.

We heard a sound in the near distance. Something opening, like an automatic door. Kelsie took out her knife.

"It's probably from one of the other houses," I said.

"What other houses?" she asked. Kelsie seemed real scared, which was troubling because she was a lot tougher than me. They call her Muscle Junkie around the neighborhood. Me, I'm just skin and bones. I'd like to say I was the brains of the operation, but I don't know.

"Let's just go a little further," I said.

After another minute, we started to hear rustling. Not all of it coming from one direction. We stopped. The sounds kept closing in on us. It didn't sound like anything large, but a thousand little machines linked to one control panel.

"Are we really here?" I asked.

"You're not that high," she responded.

We stared at each other for about a second before we ran back the way we came. Whatever we heard out there picked up its pace. It sounded like it was right on our heels and moving ahead of us on both sides. I was about ten yards in front of Kelsie.

I could see the outline of the perimeter wall. I made it to the door, but it was locked. I shook the handle and then turned to my right to see if there was a way out along the wall.

They started coming out of the bushes and trees on both sides of me. At least a dozen of each. They were everywhere. Familiar, but not the same as I'd ever seen them. Raccoons and squirrels intermingling like a fucking squadron.

"Run," I screamed, sprinting back away from the wall.

Up ahead on the path, more of them emerged from the wild vegetation, cutting us off. It was an ambush. The animals were at my heels. They surrounded Kelsie and she was soon swallowed up in a blanket of critters, working together and tearing away at her. She cried out. There were so many of them I couldn't get near her. They completely ignored me. Not one bite. I saw a lot of red, but it could've been their blood. Kelsie was quick with her knife.

Someone whistled behind me and when I looked back, the door was open. I could hear Kelsie screaming as I ran away. Once I got outside the property, I was grabbed from behind and thrown into the back of the van. We drove off.

When I got out of the van, we were in a parking lot with only one car. I knew the area. We weren't close to anything but abandoned warehouses and maybe some squatters who didn't want to be seen. The man in the passenger seat of the car was the man with the nice sunglasses from the day before. I walked over, too dry and full of varmint fear to devise an escape.

"It all went wrong," I said. "We never made it to the house. There were so many of them. She's still there."

"Did you wear the masks?" he asked.

"Yeah," I answered, bewildered by the question.

He handed me an envelope full of cash.

"But we didn't get the egg."

"You tried your best," he said. "No one could have foreseen such a thing. You deserve this for your trouble."

I looked at the money.

"They're eating her," I said.

"Maybe she got out," he said. "We'll go back and look for her. It's the least we could do. You've done enough already."

"We never even saw a house," I said.

"It's a large estate," he said, calmly. "And my parents fancy themselves horticulturalists."

The car drove away, and the van followed, leaving me stranded. I walked nine miles to our neighborhood and scored as much morsel as I could with the money.

I think that was at least a day ago, maybe more. I zoned out for a while, so it's hard to tell. Still no sign of Kelsie, but I've been wearing her clothes to remind myself to keep an eye out for her. They're a little baggy on me. The morsel is pretty much gone from my system. Sadly, I lost some of the flood to sleep.

I'll start with just a pinch from her half. If she makes it back to me, she won't know how much I got, not exactly. I'll tell her I couldn't find Izzy and had to go with some rando who has higher prices. I'll comment on how good it is though. She'll understand—even if she knows I'm lying. I'll give her everything that's left over and tell her to take it all. Unless she wants to share. It's always more fun when we get wet together.

ARMSTRONG

1. He Knows if You've Been Bad or Good

Galactic Safety Lieutenant Goric presented his gift of Earth gold to the Flagodrian chief, placing the precious metal in its tendril-paw. All was now well between the two species.

Goric looked up to thank the real hero, but Armstrong was nowhere in sight. If that dog hadn't mimicked the Flagodrian body language to teach him how they communicate, there would never have been a peaceful alliance.

The cargo shuttle launched and soon left the planet's atmosphere, heading back to the transport ship Penelope, which would then travel to Space Station Olympus to pick up more supplies. The pilot and her navigator sat back and relaxed once Penelope's tractor beam had engaged and locked onto the shuttle.

"I can't wait for Olympus," the pilot said. "It's been too long. I miss strawberry ice cream."

"Chocolate is my favorite," the navigator said. "With astro sprinkles!"

The camera leaves the cockpit, moving through the shuttle and stopping when it reaches Armstrong. He's hiding behind a large crate and looking out the window at the planet where he just saved his new friends from imminent war. His tail wags.

Armstrong paces around until he finds the right spot and lies down, closing his eyes for some well-deserved rest.

[The credits roll.]

[When the credits end, a loud commercial begins.]

Four young children run around a yard laughing. The theme song to The Little Starchaser is playing.

"Let's play with Armstrong!" A boy shouts.

"What do you mean, silly?" A girl says. "He's only on TV."

"Yeah, silly!" The other children shout together, laughing at the boy.

"Armstrong!" The boy calls out. Armstrong the dog enters and runs over to the boy. All of the other children are in awe and jump up and down with excitement.

"How did you get Armstrong?" The girl asks.

"My parents bought him for me," the boy answers. "Your parents can buy you an Armstrong too, thanks to Phyla!"

As the children run around the yard with Armstrong, the volume of their laughter and The Little Starchaser theme song lowers.

"The Real Armstrong!" A male voice-over announces. "Brought to you by Phyla from the small screen to your living room. Now, every boy and girl can have their very own Armstrong! Please visit our website at phylatechnologies.com for more details."

The camera zooms in on the boy who has his arms around the dog.

"Armstrong," the boy says, pulling the dog closer for a hug, "you're my favorite!"

Brett turned off the television, wishing he'd done so before the commercial started. The Radolinski family always watched *The Little Starchaser* together. It was Eliza's favorite show and of all the popular children's programming available, it was the show Brett and Heather enjoyed the most. Every Tuesday morning a new episode would start streaming and that night, after dinner, they would watch it with milk and cookies.

"Can I have a Armstrong?" Eliza asked. "For Christmas."

"*An* Armstrong," Heather corrected. "We'll have to think about it, sweetie."

"Please," Eliza said, looking from parent to parent to uncover her sympathizer, which varied depending on the day and the request. "I won't ask for anything else."

"It's not just about what we want," Heather said, casting an eye towards Brett. "It's about what Armstrong wants. We don't even know if he'd be happy here. Right, Brett?"

"Yeah," he responded. He took a knee to be down at eye level with his daughter. "Armstrong brings so much joy to so many children all over the world. He might not be able to if he was living in our apartment. We can't hog all of his attention."

Brett made some pig snorting noises and pushed up the tip of nose in an attempt to break up the conversation. Eliza usually loved his animal sounds.

"Not TV Armstrong," Eliza said. "I want my own Armstrong. They're different, but both real Armstrongs. There can be more of him and one of him can always be TV Armstrong."

"It's not that simple," Heather said to her daughter. "We'll try to work something out. Think about what else you might want for Christmas. But right now, it's time for somebody to brush their teeth and go to bed."

"Okay," Eliza said. Her tone wasn't angry, but sad. She walked to the bathroom, shoulders down. She usually loved her electric toothbrush. The sound and vibrations made it a perfect stand-in space tool, which she'd use on her imaginary adventures with Armstrong. He was the hero and she the intergalactic engineer whose unrecognized technical knowhow often saved the day. Armstrong always tried to give her equal credit, but his barking praise fell on deaf ears—except with the Lycanotrytes. They could speak Earth-dog.

Brett picked her up from the step stool in front of the sink, as he always did, and carried her to bed, pretending to be a shuttle. He'd talk in his softest and most soothing voice to mimic the way spaceships' computers spoke on science fiction shows and movies. Once she was in bed, Brett and Heather would tuck her in together.

Brett would make laser sounds when the overhead lights were switched off, revealing a glow-in-the-dark night sky on her ceiling. Among the constellations and planets was a dog riding a comet.

Eliza would say, "Good night, Armstrong." Then, her parents would respond, "Ruff ruff, ruff ruff."

But, for the first time since the ritual began, she just closed her eyes and went to sleep without a word.

Brett and Heather went online that night to find out exactly what this Armstrong-dog was and how much it would set them back if they were to buy it for Eliza as a Christmas gift. According to the Phyla website, the company was selling clones of the real Armstrong from the television show. They had engineered the original Armstrong and retained the exclusive reproductive cloning rights for the dog's DNA. When *The Little Starchaser* was renewed for five more seasons by PrimeFlix, Phyla immediately began production on the first batch. Only a limited number of the young adult Armstrongs were available, but there were also portions of the one-year-old and newborn puppy generations for sale. If those sold out, consumers had the option of paying to have a new clone produced, which was priced higher because it was considered a custom order. These different prices were irrelevant to Brett and Heather. The cheapest Armstrong was the cost of four months' rent.

"There's just no way," Heather said to Brett, who was poring over their finances, hoping to find a forgotten pocket of savings or some way to move their meager resources around in order to make Eliza's Christmas wish come true. He knew it was useless, but the foolish optimist in him could never be washed away entirely. Heather indulged him because she felt his wishful spirit was good for family morale.

"The look on her face," Brett said, looking up from the spreadsheet.

"I know," Heather agreed, leaning in and kissing the side of his forehead. "It kills me too. But we're drowning as it is. We need to figure out how we're going to handle the debt we already have."

Brett smiled at her, close-lipped, and then minimized the spreadsheet. Eliza was almost eight years old and in her second year of a tier-one educational sponsorship provided by Jupiter Industries, which bound her to work for ten years as an employee of the company after she'd completed her education. It had been a dream come true when they received her sponsorship acceptance letter. There would be so many career options for her with a tier-one at such a large and well-respected company. It would be a sea change for the family.

A year into Eliza's schooling was when the material costs started piling up. Things like a digital tablet with specific educational software and lab equipment were required and costly. They'd been under the impression that materials would be provided for and all expenses would be covered by the sponsorship, but after the first year, only tuition and lunches were included. Jupiter Industries offered financial loans to cover any other educational expenses. Each loan was for twenty-thousand dollars and the annual interest was an additional three months of contracted labor for Eliza as an employee of Jupiter Industries. They had just taken out their second loan, which meant Eliza was accruing an additional year of contracted labor for every two years that passed by until the Radolinskis completely paid off the loans. As it was, she'd be working for Jupiter Industries into her late thirties.

It was a good company to work for and perhaps Eliza would never want to work anywhere else. But, if she ever felt compelled to take her life in a different direction, she wouldn't be able to do so until she'd completed the terms of her sponsorship contract.

"It's not as if I thought I was going to find a way," Brett said to Heather as he followed her into their bedroom. "I guess I just wanted to be able to tell myself I tried."

Heather loved him. Sometimes he made her want to scream.

2. It's the Most Wonderful Time of the Year

Eddie Carbone had never fully adjusted to life on Space Station Olympus. It was so far from any other large Intergalactic Peace Confederation bases or stations that it served as a major hub and layover for hundreds of different alien species and planets.

It had been four years since he left Earth. He missed Newark. He missed being surrounded by a majority of humans. Mostly, he missed his family, especially around the holidays.

But he couldn't pass up the business opportunity. "Carbone's at Olympus" was the only pizzeria in the middle of twelve heavily trafficked galaxies and his ticket to early retirement. It was a taste of home for mankind and a delicious new curiosity for the universe at large. The business was so popular, he made fifty times the amount he had selling slices back home. He was able to buy his parents a place with an indoor swimming pool and everything.

Still, he hated living on Olympus. He figured ten more years and he could retire early. It was hard spending Christmas surrounded by all of the "space weirdos." That's what he called them, to their faces. Even the ones who were nice to him. Even Thlakti, a young Cephaladassian boy who idolized Eddie. His parents owned and operated an interspecies medical supply store on Olympus, but Thlakti wanted to grow up to be a pizza maker just like his hero. Eddie could never get past the tentacles.

When he came into work on Christmas Eve and saw the slimy pile of space fungus on his prep counter contaminating his toppings, he was furious. Thlakti was inside the shop smiling at Eddie. Convinced Thlakti had just pranked him, Eddie chased the boy out of the shop, yelling at him never to come back. Thlakti ran as fast as he could, staining his new white shirt with streams of black ink tears. Eddie was about to clean up the mess the boy had left for him, but instead threw his towel at the wall. He sat down on the floor, miserable and homesick, wondering if he'd been too harsh. Armstrong had witnessed the whole thing and walked over to Eddie, licking his hand. Eddie scratched behind the dog's ears.

About a half hour later, Thlakti's parents came looking for him. He was supposed to run an errand for them and come right home. Eddie told them Thlakti had pulled a prank on him and he'd yelled at their son, adding that maybe he overdid it. They apologized for their son's behavior, remarking how it was so unlike him. Armstrong barked at them and then at the pizza counter. They all looked confused. Armstrong stood up, placing his paws on the counter, barking towards Thlakti's space fungus. They all walked around to the other side of the counter.

"It's Thlakti's Fartokian Onculyx!" the father said. Black ink started running down the mother's face.

"That doesn't sound like a pile of space sludge," Eddie said.

"It's similar to what you Earth-humans would call a pet," the father explained. "But rare and quite valuable. Only the luckiest Cephaladassian children receive them as gifts. It's Thlakti's most prized possession."

"Why would he have just left it on my counter?" Eddie asked.

"It's a gift," the mother answered, black ink dripping from her chin. Eddie handed her a napkin to wipe it off. "Yesterday, he told me he needed to give you something very special for Earth Christmas because you were so lonely for your family. I just didn't imagine he would give you something he cherished so much."

"And I scolded him for it," Eddie said, disgusted with himself. "Poor little guy. Where does he go when he's really upset?"

"He likes the solitude and echoes of the old garbage expulsion tubes," the father said. "Ever since we've switched to recycling thermulators, those tubes have been abandoned and unused."

"What time is it?" Eddie asked.

"Fifteen-fifty," the father answered. "Why?"

"The Earth residents are planning to launch two tons of white confetti out of those tubes at sixteen-hundred so it will look like snow for Christmas Eve," Eddie said. "We've got to get him out of there."

Eddie ran towards the old garbage tubes. Armstrong sprinted ahead and started barking when he found the boy. Thlakti had slipped into one of the lower chambers of the garbage tube system and got his foot stuck in one of the gears to a conveyer belt. The belt began to move, dragging Thlakti with the piles of confetti. Eddie jumped down and managed to free the boy's foot. He handed Thlakti up towards Armstrong, who clenched his teeth onto the waist of the boy's pants and pulled him to safety. Seconds after Eddie climbed up out of the expulsion tube, the bags of confetti were released into space. The little bits of *paper created a snow-globe effect in front of the upper deck viewing bay for five seconds before they dispersed into the darkness.*

"I'm sorry I yelled at you," Eddie said. "I didn't realize that Fracktobrian Bonkulax was so special."

"Fartokian Onculyx!" Thlakti corrected him, laughing as he wiped the ink from his eyes. "I just wanted to make Earth Christmas special for you."

"You know, Thlakti," Eddie said. It was the first time he'd addressed the boy by his name. "Christmas is about family and I miss my Earth family a whole lot, but maybe it's time I started appreciating my Olympus family too."

Eddie put his hand on Thlakti's shoulder, and the boy hugged Eddie with all of his arms and tentacles.

"Now, how about we go back to the shop and start cooking my favorite holiday meal," Eddie said. "The Feast of the Seven Pizzas!"

Thlakti jumped up and Armstrong barked enthusiastically.

"You said it, Pal," Eddie responded, taking Thlakti's hand as all three of them walked away together. "Happy Christmas to all, and to all a good night."

[The credits roll to The Little Starchaser theme song with sleigh bell sounds playing along with the normal tune.]

Heather turned off the television. This was the second year in a row *The Little Starchaser* aired a holiday special on Christmas Eve. Eliza was struggling to keep her eyes open and was fast asleep by the time Brett carried her to the bathroom, so they skipped their end of the night dental hygiene ritual and put her straight to bed.

When Heather woke up the next morning, Brett wasn't next to her. Eliza was already sitting next to the artificial Christmas tree inspecting the size of her gifts and picking them up to feel their weight. She tried to mask her disappointment with a forced smile to her mother.

"Merry Christmas," Heather said. "Where's your father?"

"I don't know," Eliza answered. "There's a note next to the Christmas cake."

Christmas cake was their holiday breakfast tradition of home-made coffee cake covered with white frosting and red and green sprinkles. The note simply said: *Merry Christmas! I won't be long. Xoxo Hohoho.* Heather put it back down on the table and looked at Eliza, who was wearing a pair of space-themed pajamas and holding her well-worn stuffed Armstrong.

"How about some cake while we wait for your father?" Heather asked.

Eliza nodded and ran over to the table and sat down at her chair, placing the stuffed Armstrong into the highchair she'd long outgrown. Heather sliced a piece of cake, of which she sliced off a third, putting the smaller slice on a plate in front of the stuffed Armstrong and the larger piece in front of Eliza.

"Armstrong wants a bigger piece," Eliza said.

"Let's start with this piece," Heather responded, raising an eyebrow at her daughter. "And if he still wants more after he's finished, then we'll talk."

A few minutes later, Brett returned and immediately shuffled into their bedroom, shouting for them to stay where they were. He walked out, poured himself a cup of coffee and kissed Heather.

"Who's ready to open presents?" he asked.

"I am," Eliza shouted and ran over to the tree, letting herself fall cross-legged to the ground.

"What's going on?" Heather asked Brett quietly, sensing some nervous energy from her husband. "You're acting strange."

"I just want her to have a good Christmas," he answered. "We can talk about this later."

"Talk about what?" She asked.

Brett was already on the floor next to Eliza by the time she finished the question. Heather was uneasy with his evasiveness, but she didn't want to ruin the morning for her daughter.

They exchanged gifts. Heather received a mystery novel she'd wanted from Eliza. Brett gave her a painting of a red fox leaping up in the air to dive headfirst into the deep powdery snow for prey. She loved collecting and looking through old National Geographic magazines. Every Christmas, Brett would paint a scene from a photo out of an issue in her collection. Her Christmas afternoon activity would be to search through all of her magazines until she found the photograph that inspired her gift and compare the two images next to each other. Brett didn't paint much anymore, but before they had Eliza and he got a job as a data analyst, he spent at least three hours a day painting.

Eliza gave Brett three new paint brushes made with real Phyla sable hair and two tubes of his favorite oil paints in cadmium red and burnt sienna. Heather gave him a large book on the Hudson

River School of painters with full color plates. She would put away a little money every month throughout the year so she could buy him a rare art book. The year before it had been the complete works of John James Audubon.

Eliza tore into her presents, which were all Armstrong-themed. An action-figure playset of a planet colony and a space shuttle. An Armstrong backpack with a matching water bottle. She looked at her parents and smiled.

"I think there's one more present in the other room," Brett said. "Let me go check."

Eliza smiled wider.

"Brett?" Heather said.

He left and came back, leading a dog on a leash. It looked like Armstrong, fully grown but younger.

"Armstrong!" Eliza screamed and ran over. The dog seemed a little skittish when she got on her knees and hugged him, but he didn't growl.

"I can't believe you did this behind my back," Heather said to Brett, trying to be quiet as she pulled him by the arm into the kitchen where Eliza wouldn't hear them as well. "What's wrong with you?"

"I know," Brett said. "I'm not asking you not to be angry with me, but it's not as bad as you think."

"We discussed this," she said without looking at him.

"He's a knock-off," he said.

"What?" Heather asked.

"He's not a Phyla clone," he answered, quietly so Eliza wouldn't hear. "He's a knockoff engineered to look like Armstrong. It was a fraction of the cost."

"How'd you pay for it?"

"I sold my father's watch."

"You loved that watch," she said, softening her tone, briefly.

"Yeah," he said. "But she deserves a happy Christmas."

"I'm really mad at you," she said.

"I'm sorry," he said, reaching out a hand. She didn't reach back, but she didn't pull away. He briefly rubbed the back of her arm and then let his hand fall to his side.

"We're not nineteen," Heather said to him. "We have a child and a lot of debt. This kind of big surprise isn't cute anymore."

Brett thought about a response.

"You deceived me," she said and walked back into the living room, breaking into a big smile for Eliza as she sat on the floor.

Eliza scratched the dog behind the ears. She was as happy as they'd ever seen her. The dog seemed indifferent to the attention and after a moment, walked into the kitchen sniffing everywhere, never sitting still for more than a few seconds. He roamed around the apartment, determined, as if he were mapping the boundaries of a new territory. Eliza's enthusiasm was unaffected by his ambivalence. She followed him around, narrating out loud the adventure she was creating for the two of them.

Later, in the middle of the night, Brett got up from the couch to go to the bathroom. Heather would eventually forgive him but needed a night or two sleeping in different rooms.

When he walked back from the bathroom through the kitchen, Brett noticed the dog standing in the entrance from the living room leading to the front hallway and bedrooms. He was panting and looking forward as if he wanted something. But, instead of running up to one of the doors or the empty dog bowl and whimpering or barking to communicate what it wanted, he just stood in place as if patiently waiting. Brett thought the dog's behavior was odd. He called out *Armstrong* in his loudest whisper.

The dog looked at him for a moment and then turned his head back, staring down the dark hallway.

Brett laid down on the couch and watched the dog for an hour or so while he checked email and read portions of news articles in a near dream state of tapping, scrolling, and refreshing. The animal remained where it was on all fours, panting. Waiting.

Eventually, Brett fell asleep and when he woke up briefly, an hour or two later, the dog had moved on and was no longer in sight.

When Heather woke up the next morning, the dog was standing outside Eliza's room, facing the door. There was no evidence of menace, but it still seemed odd the way he was lingering. She shooed him away and checked to make sure the door was fully closed and couldn't be pushed open. The dog eagerly followed her into the kitchen and devoured the food she poured out for him before she had time to finish making coffee.

3. Said the Night Wind to the Little Lamb

Ensign Sandra Kim had never been part of an Intergalactic Peace Confederation first contact envoy before. She'd only joined the crew of the IPC Athena starship fifteen months earlier and her probationary period had been spent training and assisting operations for several departments on board. This first planetary mission was both terrifying and exhilarating to her.

The highest-ranking officer on this exploratory mission was Galactic Safety Lieutenant Brock Landers. Sandra found him arrogant and impetuous, always focused on his own glory and never on building relationships in service of intergalactic peace. IPC Protocol clearly stated that, upon landing on the surface of an unexplored planet displaying signs of intelligent life, the first contact envoy was to remain within a twenty-yard radius of the shuttle for no shorter than twelve hours to allow the dominant and intelligent native species to introduce themselves and approach first. All galactic psychological research studies suggested this approach made the intruding group appear less threatening. But Brock Landers would only wait an hour before he ordered the surface team to move out and explore the planet.

It was not unheard of for surface teams to have dogs accompany them, but Sandra had never seen this dog before and there was no mention of a dog on the shuttle's manifest for this mission. She would normally bring this to the attention of a higher-ranking officer, but considering Brock Landers' reckless departure strategy, Sandra felt more comfortable having an IPC dog's honed senses to warn them of danger, even if it wasn't officially supposed to be on the mission. She also thought it abnormal the dog wasn't wearing an official IPC badge, but only a tag with its name: Armstrong.

Armstrong stayed close to Sandra, sensing she was the wisest and most fit to lead this expedition. When he heard something moving in on them, he tried to get her attention without barking. Sandra could tell something was wrong.

"I think we're in danger," she said. "Armstrong is acting strange."

"That dog hasn't barked once," Brock Landers responded. "Stop interfering with the progress of this mission. Do I need to remind you who's in charge here, ensign?"

"No, Lieutenant" she answered.

"Good," he said. "If there are any further interruptions, you might not be recommended to go on a second planetary surface mission."

Armstrong began whimpering to Sandra while pointing his head in every direction.

"Will you shut that dog up, Ensign," Brock Landers ordered.

Before the surface team took one more step, ferocious creatures leapt out of the bushes from every direction, completely surrounding the team and outnumbering them at least five-to-one. They walked on two legs like humans, but they were very large and muscular, covered in dark brown fur with dog-like features. To Sandra, they looked similar to the werewolves she'd seen in movies and on television and described in books of supernatural fiction. They were terrifying, claws protracted *and drool forming like stalactites at the tips of their fangs.*

A chorus of vicious growls surrounding them, the surface team took out their plasma rifles and hand blasters, arranging themselves into a tactical circle formation.

"I am Galactic Safety Lieutenant Brock Landers. We are representatives of the Intergalactic Peace Confederation, here to introduce ourselves in hopes of building an alliance."

"Garrrrrrrrrrr," the wolf-alien who appeared to be the leader of the wolf-aliens growled out. Slightly quieter and lesser growls were made in response.

"We mean you no harm," Brock Landers shouted. "But I will order my team to open fire on yours if you don't back away!"

Just as the wolf-alien leader lowered his pose as if he was getting ready to pounce forward, Armstrong ran straight up to him and started barking.

"That dog's going to get us all killed!" Brock Landers yelled.

But the wolf-alien leader didn't become aggravated or further angered by Armstrong's barks. Instead, he looked at the dog with a calm concentration as if he were listening to what Armstrong was saying. After a minute, the two began barking back and forth with each other.

"What's happening?" Brock Landers asked. He sounded confused and resentful.

"I think they're communicating with each other, sir," Sandra answered.

"You think?" Brock Landers said, sarcastically.

The wolf-alien leader growled out to his pack and they eased out of their attack postures. He straightened up and faced the IPC surface team, suddenly looking more regal than bellicose.

"Garrrrr. I am Lupinecanis Lobo and I am Supreme Chieftain of the Lycanotrytes. I am known, commonly, as Chief Lobo and I welcome you to Remoria."

Brock Landers began to introduce himself, but Chief Lobo raised his paw-hand to interrupt.

"Silence," Chief Lobo ordered. "We will consider a peaceful truce with your intrusion pack, but I will only speak and negotiate with Armstrong and the one you call Sandrakim."

"You can't order me around," Brock Landers responded. "I'm the leader of this IPC mission. You'll speak to me or you'll speak to no one!"

The rest of the surface team looked at each other, scared and upset with Landers for aggravating the tense situation.

"With one single howl, garrrrr, I can have hundreds of my warriors descend upon you within seconds," Chief Lobo said with an unwavering confidence. "It would be bloody and quick. You would all perish. Or…you can agree to my terms and step away."

Brock Landers looked at Chief Lobo and the rest of his pack and then back to his surface team. He was furious, but instead of lashing out as he desperately wanted to, he stepped back, clenching his jaw. He understood the reality of the situation and how any physical confrontation would play out.

Sandra approached the Lycanotrytes and put out her hand. Chief Lobo looked at her exposed palm and then to Armstrong, who barked four times. Chief Lobo shook her hand.

"Armstrong speaks very highly of you."

"You understand him that well?" Sandra asked, smiling at Armstrong.

"Yes," Chief Lobo answered. "We Lycanotrytes are naturally great warriors, but our greatest gift lies in our born-in-blood ability to understand languages. We often decipher new languages as fast as they are spoken to us. Your earth-dog is similar to our root tongue, making it especially intuitive for our ears."

"What does Armstrong have to say about us?" Sandra asked.

"Well," Chief said, pondering his next words for a moment. "He says on every ship of fools throughout the galaxies, there is one wise person and that is who one should first seek to find. He also stated though earth-humans are terrible at diplomacy, many of them genuinely want to help and bring peace to the galaxies."

"Oh," Sandra responded. She was confused and unsure of what to make of Armstrong's thoughts.

"He told me you are his friend," Chief Lobo said, placing his paw-hand on her shoulder. "And I can trust you."

Sandra looked down at Armstrong and scratched him behind the ears. Armstrong barked eight times.

Chief Lobo started grunting and chuckling, which soon turned into a laughing howl so infectious it spread to all of his soldiers and then beyond. Within thirty seconds, thousands upon thousands of Lycano-trytes howled for miles throughout the Remorian woods. It sounded like echoes in an endless cave.

[The credits roll.]

———————

Brett turned off the television. It was nearly seven and their guests would be arriving soon. They'd celebrated every New Year's Eve for the past five years with the Bells and the Mendozas, rotating between the three households.

"Can't I watch one more?" Eliza moaned, holding her old stuffed Armstrong.

"You've already watched two," Brett said. They'd let her watch twice the normal daily allotment on New Year's Eve. This first appearance of the Lycanotrytes was her favorite episode of the show and she'd seen it at least forty times.

"It's time to get ready for our guests," Heather said. "And you're old enough to help us clean up. It can be fun. You and Armstrong can make up an adventure out of it."

Eliza looked over at her Christmas present, which was pant-ing and staring at the oven, eagerly waiting for the large roast of

Phylanthium Farms pork shoulder to be put back on the counter. Eliza had never wanted anything so badly in her life, but it wasn't how she imagined it would be. They were supposed to be friends like Armstrong and Sandra Kim, travelling the galaxies and saving the day together—a storyline that had played out hundreds of times in Eliza's imagination.

But *her* Armstrong never wanted to play and his indifference to human affection was heart-breaking. The way he would follow her around the apartment, but never move in close to be pet or roll over to have his belly scratched made her feel like she was being evaluated, not loved.

Eliza wished she'd never asked for the dog or could send him back. But she knew returning him wasn't an option. "No refunds" flashed across the screen several times during every advertisement for the cloned Armstrongs. Plus, she didn't want to disappoint her parents. She'd overheard them talking about how expensive he was one night when they thought she was sleeping.

"Okay," Eliza said, trying to muster some cheer as she began to pick up her toys. "Come on, Armstrong! It's time to fill up the recycling thermulators."

Eliza began to pick up her toys around the living room. In her head, she was thinking of ways to get rid of Armstrong without hurting him and also make it look like an accident. She could set him free and tell her parents she'd tried to take him for a walk, then he overpowered her and got away. She didn't hate the dog. He wasn't mean to her, but she knew as long as he stayed, she'd have to pretend she was excited about him.

Armstrong was still in the kitchen pacing back and forth in front of the oven the way a tiger might pace along a glass enclosure wall at the zoo, trying to find a way out to get at the human spectators.

Heather saw the disappointment in her daughter's posture and movements and was familiar with the cadence of Eliza's voice when she was pretending to be happy. She knew their daughter just wanted them to think she was grateful for the gift they'd given her. A gift that was a lie. He wasn't the cloned Armstrong Eliza had seen on TV and begged for. He was a false blend. Eliza had sacrificed futures she wasn't even aware of yet. Futures shed so she would be able to care for Heather and Brett in their old age. Futures she wouldn't be able to choose for herself. Futures forced upon her. And, here she was, feigning contentment to spare her parents' feelings.

Heather felt sick. They were all lying to each other. Eliza to her parents so they wouldn't be upset with her. Brett to all of them, including himself, acting as if he could provide them with privileges that he didn't have access to. And Heather, trying to convince herself she was raising her daughter as if it were a selfless act.

Heather looked over into the kitchen at the strange dog. The way he motioned and held his body disturbed her. His appearance seemed identical to Armstrong with its sheer black coat and shape and size—a mixture of wolfdog components like Siberian Husky or German Shepherd, perhaps some Alaskan Malamute to make it a little thicker. But these attributes only accounted for the aesthetics of his appearance and not behavior. Even though she'd never had a dog before, Heather had watched a lot of nature documentaries and felt their Armstrong was different from the average domestic dog. She wasn't worried as much as cautious around the dog. He seemed trapped between two worlds. He wagged his tail here and there. Sometimes he listened to commands. He would occasionally sit when told to sit and cower when told a harsh no, but other times it was as though he couldn't hear the emotional tone in their voices.

Shortly after Eliza went to bed, the guests arrived. Chuck and

Adeline Bell brought their dog with them—a Bichon Frisé named Mr. Ruffles. They never left him home alone. While Adeline set down the snack food they brought with them for the pre-dinner cocktail hour, Chuck released Mr. Ruffles from his leash. The small dog immediately ran up to Armstrong, yipping with authority, but the larger dog was still focused so purely on the slow-roasting pork shoulder in the oven, he barely noticed his challenger.

Henry and Ted Mendoza left their two young daughters, Rita and Diana, at home with a babysitter. They provided six bottles of expensive champagne for the evening. All three couples had known each other for over a decade. Heather and Brett had gone to college with Adeline and Henry. The four of them had become inseparable after Heather and Brett started dating sophomore year, and they'd stayed close ever since.

"How are the girls?" Heather asked.

"They're great," Henry said. "Their personalities are really starting to break away from each other. Rita is endlessly curious, and Diana is definitely the creative member of the family. You should hear her voice."

"How's Eliza doing in school?" Ted asked.

"Straight A's," Heather answered, proudly.

"She's the smartest among us," Ted said and meant it. "I've been telling Henry it's high time our girls started taking their education more seriously."

"They're only five and six," Henry said directly to his husband. "I just want to let them be kids a little longer. They have a lifetime to be serious."

Ted glared at Henry, who immediately understood what his husband was communicating. They'd both been extremely successful in their careers. Henry was vice president of marketing for the domestic and recreational division of Phyla's sales department and Ted had been with Terracom Inc. for a decade, working his way up to assistant director of acquisitions for the northeast region. They were the rare parents who could afford to pay for their children's education without the aid of a sponsorship or a drastic change in their lifestyle. They were both sensitive to this privilege and generous with their friends and families. But sometimes a comment would slip, accidental and with no ill intentions, pointing out the disparities between theirs and the lives of others. As innocent as a statement about not wanting young children to have to worry too much about their academic standings.

"But I always end up deferring to Ted on these issues," Henry said with a warm smile. "If it were up to me, the girls would never do their homework if they didn't want to."

"Tell me about it," Ted said, looking at Heather and rolling his eyes towards Henry as he popped the cork on the first bottle of the night. Heather winked back at him. She handed out flutes as Ted poured. Adeline walked around offering bacon-wrapped dates to everyone while Chuck got Mr. Ruffles a little bowl of water.

After the first toast and sip, Henry peeked over at Armstrong, inquisitively. He was dubious, having seen many of the clones firsthand at work while Phyla was developing the marketing campaign. But he kept these observations to himself.

"You bit the bullet and got an Armstrong for Eliza," Henry said. "She must have been over the moon."

"Yeah," Brett responded. "It's all she wanted. I had to sell my father's antique watch to help pay for him."

"I think it's an unnatural creature," Adeline said. She'd long been anti-cloning for non-endangered species, which created some tension with Henry.

"Mr. Ruffles wasn't exactly born in the wild," Henry shot back.

"He descends from water dogs used for hunting," Adeline responded, defensively. "And Spanish sailing dogs. He has a long history."

"And I descend from cavemen," Henry said, looking at Heather and Ted with a champagne grin. "But I still can't start a fire without a match."

It was hard not to laugh. Henry was very funny when he was tipsy. Not as much when he was drunk. Even Adeline couldn't suppress a little chuckle.

"I just think it's weird cloning a celebrity animal," Adeline said. "It's like you're buying a character and not a pet. What's the future hold for us? Will everyone have clones of celebrities to keep as live-in sex toys?"

"You say that like it's a bad thing," Henry said, giggling at his own words. "Sadly, I think we're still a long way from that happening. Besides, what celebrity would voluntarily submit themselves to a procedure that ensured they were no longer one of a kind?"

Everybody laughed and kept drinking and nibbling at the snacks. Henry and Adeline continued their playful debate. They'd always shared an antagonistic chemistry.

Heather was glad the conversation had taken on a life of its own and veered away from her and Brett explaining their decision to buy the cloned dog. When she thought about it, she still became angry that he'd made the decision to get the dog without her.

Brett took out the pork roast, which meant it would be ready to eat in about twenty minutes. While the guests were distracting themselves with alcohol and laughter, Heather finished setting the table and Brett prepared the side dishes.

By the time dinner ended and everyone retired from the table to the couches, it was about an hour and a half until midnight. Brett could see Mr. Ruffles rolling on his back so someone, anyone, would scratch his belly. But Armstrong was nowhere in sight.

Brett was a dog person. He'd grown up in a house where there were always one or two rescue mutts and they'd come in all sizes and temperaments. Often a pit bull or some other pariah breed. His parents believed they deserved a loving home as much as any dog. Yet, there was something about the knockoff Armstrong that made him want to know where he was at all times. That's why he walked to the front hallway where the bedrooms were to make sure everything was okay. He'd never felt this way about a dog before. He'd never been worried about their behavior.

He found Armstrong just outside of Eliza's bedroom, digging at the floor near the bottom of the door. He snapped at the dog as quietly as he could, trying not to draw attention from the other room. He told Armstrong to get away from the door. The dog looked at him, unfazed by the disciplinary tone. Brett continued to scold the dog until he turned away and walked back towards the kitchen and living room.

Brett looked down at the floor where Armstrong had been scratching. There were visible marks in the wood as if the dog were trying to dig his way under the door into Eliza's room. Brett quietly opened the door and entered. Eliza was sleeping peacefully in her bed, unaware of the activity in the hallway. Brett leaned up against the wall, watching her. He wished he didn't need sleep and could stand guard all night. He saw a plate of cookies half-hidden under her bed and wondered if that's what Armstrong had been after.

A loud yelp reverberated throughout the apartment. Somebody screamed in the living room, but it didn't wake Eliza. Brett left the room, closing the door behind him and checking twice to confirm it was secure. He ran back down the hallway towards the sounds of commotion. In the middle of the living room was Heather, kneeling with blood on her arms and shirt. Adeline was standing with a whimpering and bloodied Mr. Ruffles in her arms. Armstrong was at the other side of the room, looking nervous with blood around his mouth and at his back ankle.

"He's a wild animal," Adeline yelled at Heather with anger boiling in her voice. "And shouldn't be around families."

"I thought you said he was unnatural," Heather snapped back, mocking Adeline.

"You know what I mean," Adeline responded, yelling even louder. "He went after Mr. Ruffles and then he bit you."

"What?" Heather shouted, standing up to face Adeline. "Mr. Ruffles attacked Armstrong. He was only defending himself when he bit back. And it was Mr. Ruffles who bit me while I was breaking them apart."

"That's a lie," Adeline said. Chuck and Henry both attempted to calm the situation, gesturing towards the bedrooms and reminding them Eliza was sleeping.

"Armstrong was minding his own business," Heather declared. "Mr. Ruffles shouldn't even be allowed off his leash."

Adeline said nothing. She looked at Heather as if a line had just been crossed and they would no longer be able to work out this issue between them.

Heather didn't know why she was suddenly so protective of Armstrong and it wasn't just because Mr. Ruffles had started the conflict. Earlier, all she could think about was how to get rid of him and now she seemed willing to end old friendships to defend his honor.

"Let's go home, Chuck," Adeline said to her husband and began walking towards the front hallway. "Happy New Year, everyone."

As Chuck gathered their things, Brett asked Ted what happened.

"Mr. Ruffles bit Armstrong on the back of the leg and Armstrong bit back" Ted said, whispering so no one else would hear. "Then Heather got between them and I guess it seems like Mr. Ruffles snapped at her, but it was hard to tell in all of the chaos."

Henry walked across the room to Ted and Brett.

"I think we should call it a night," Henry interjected. They said their goodbyes and walked out behind Chuck.

Brett went over to Heather, who had gone into the kitchen and returned. She drizzled a little red wine over a small blood stain on the carpet, then rubbed it in with a dish cloth. She still hadn't tended to her own wound.

"Are you ok?" he asked.

She nodded.

"What are you doing?" he asked.

"I'll never get this stain out tonight and I don't want Eliza to know it's blood," Heather responded as if there was nothing abnormal in her actions. "She'll sniff the stain out of curiosity in the morning, so we need to be sure it smells of nothing but wine."

"Ok," Brett said, kissing the top of her head and rubbing her back. "But then let's disinfect your wound and bandage it up."

Brett looked over at Armstrong cowering in the corner of the room. A dog, new and unfamiliar to his surroundings, taken away from all he had ever known and placed with strangers who had already decided who he was going to be and how he was going to behave and what they were going to mean to him.

Armstrong walked slowly across the room, his head lowered, and laid down under the dining table. His nose was pointed away from Brett and Heather, but his eyes looked back towards them.

THE SALT BOX

PART ONE: BUNKER 15C

The osprey hovered in the sky above the evergreen canopy, flapping its wings to hold itself in place, treading air like water. It looked straight down, patiently, and dove towards the dark blue-green lake.

Winthrop sipped his coffee, Aztec Blend with powdered milk, then switched to a ground-level view on the wall screen. The osprey crashed through the water and emerged with empty talons. The weight of its wetness brought it back down towards the lake, so it flapped harder to lighten its load.

Winthrop switched to a wide-angle view of the lake and the forest to watch the osprey fly up above the trees, letting the wind dry its feathers while it searched for a new target. He turned up the outdoor ambient wind volume and sat down at his workstation to check all the systems and look over his itinerary for the day. He'd just downloaded and installed Virtually Nature on his media processor the week before. As a boy, Winthrop dreamed of living in a cabin on a lake in a forest, far away from any city. Virtually Nature not only reproduced the images and sounds of his chosen environment, it also recreated the appropriate temperature and humidity and shot beams of replicated sunlight throughout the bunker, moving the shadows as the day went on. The olfactory diffuser was on the Vermont Fireplace setting. Whenever he went to the bathroom and closed the door, he'd bury his nose in his shirt sleeve, which smelled of wood smoke.

In the beginning, morning had been the worst part of the day in the bunker. Waking up and opening his eyes to the realization it had not all been a terrible dream was a subtle kind of torture. As days turned into weeks and weeks into months, the shock of his new existence began to wear off. Mornings became his favorite time of day because they represented new beginnings and the possibility of transformation. He could tell himself maybe today was the day he'd be freed from his manmade cocoon, the day the air above ground would be breathable again. But, after an hour or so, he'd surrender himself to reality and embrace the day, fighting torpor with daily routines and tasks.

There were moments when he felt reassured in his convictions. After years of having his fears and anxieties dismissed as paranoia and delusion, the world had proved him right. He'd been told it was a coordinated attack. Chemical and biological weapons had been released across the planet, making the already compromised atmosphere uninhabitable for human life. Everything happened so fast, Winthrop never found out who was behind it and there was nobody left on the Earth's surface to report back what had happened.

It was Wednesday in the bunker, which meant taking a full inventory of supplies until 4pm. Then at 5:30pm he'd have one of his biweekly chats with Sophia and Derek from Bunker 15B. They were the only other survivors Winthrop had been in contact with since he entered 15C. But he'd calculated if there was a consistent numbering system and each number had an A, B, & C with a two-person capacity per bunker, there were at least seventy-eight more potential survivors, and that's only if the numbers stopped at fifteen, the letters at C, and none of them had more than two occupants. There could be hundreds or even thousands of people living underground. Or maybe it was just the three of them.

But Winthrop was alone. There were two sleeping quarters, one with his name on the door and the other for a woman named Mindy Bloomfield, but she never made it to Bunker 15C. It was clear the bunker had been stocked and customized for two particular people. Much of the space seemed as though it had been designed specifically with him in mind, but then there were many features and objects selected for someone with different tastes. This was most evident in the two companion dolls. One was a female doll, designed as an exact replica of Penelope Lorenza, an actress Winthrop had been infatuated with from the time he was eleven. She was the celebrity crush of his life. The doll was the spitting image of Penelope at the age of twenty-eight when she starred in the film *Dangerous Connections* as a cyber-hacker named Warbird. The other doll was male, well-proportioned and conventionally attractive, but Winthrop couldn't identify a single distinguishing characteristic. It seemed like a blank canvas of a companion doll. Sometimes Winthrop caught himself staring at the male doll, wondering if he was better off alone in the bunker without Mindy Bloomfield, convinced that the person who the male doll had been designed for couldn't be very interesting.

When he was particularly lonely, Winthrop would pretend he and Penelope were sharing the bunker with a really boring and condescending gentleman named Ned Williams. They would always take each other's side against Ned. It made Winthrop feel there was someone in the bunker more alone than he was. Then he'd realize what he was doing, what he was wishing upon another person, and hate himself for it. It didn't matter that Ned didn't exist, only that Winthrop wanted Ned to exist and wanted him to be lonely.

The ensuing depression usually lasted for a couple days. Those were some of his lowest points in the bunker, the pockets of time between his cruel fantasies and the next video chat with Sophia and Derek. Sophia made him feel better about himself.

Winthrop finished the cup of coffee, then swirled his index finger around the inside of the mug to wipe away the residue. He avoided using water to clean his dishes and drinkware whenever possible, but he didn't like the dried residue mixed with his fresh coffee the next day. He thought it gave the coffee a stale sour taste. After he sucked his finger and dried it off in his hair, he picked up his inventory clipboard and went to the storage room.

The living quarters were the size and layout of a 1200-square-foot two-bedroom apartment, but the storage space was at least twice that size—meant to hold a lifetime's worth of supplies living in the bunker and also a stockpile of what would be necessary to start from scratch above ground. Winthrop didn't need to take a weekly inventory. He was the only person using the supplies, so he could just keep track of what he'd used up and subtract it from the list. But it busied his thoughts and hands for an entire day. Any distraction from the stillness and solitude of the bunker was a small victory.

Winthrop would start with the supplies meant for survival above ground because they were kept in the back of the storage room. He liked moving systematically forward towards the entrance. If he could see a doorway ahead, then he knew there were places to go.

First, the small refrigerator of heirloom seeds—broken up into two major groups, which Winthrop differentiated as culinary and non-edibles. The first group consisted of hundreds of seeds for vegetables, fruits, legumes, cereals, tubers, and herbs. Every time he counted them all and took stock, Winthrop imagined the entire history of human agriculture before him. The non-edibles were seeds for trees, flowers, succulents, and grasses. A bookcase next to the refrigerator included several books on farming and horticulture, brewing ales, winemaking, distilling spirits, fermentation, pickling, cheese-making, curing meats and fish, making food oils, drying spices and herbs, and making salt. Spore prints for mushrooms and moss spores were kept separately in sealed plastic bags in their own small refrigerator. Winthrop worried the spores would be ruined somehow before he left the bunker and the new world would only know the taste of mushrooms if there were some leftover dried specimens from the food pantries meant for life inside the bunkers. So, he never ate any from his supply. He saved them for life after the bunker. He'd urged Sophia and Derek to do the same. She suggested the possibility that, in the absence of an active human civilization in the outside world, animal and plant life might thrive, but also promised they would cut down on their dried mushroom consumption. When he finished going over the heirloom seeds, he checked to make sure the storage space dehumidifier was operating correctly.

Winthrop wasn't a religious man, but he often prayed there was a massive underground facility somewhere serving as Noah's ark with two of every animal for the future world above. He feared a world where humans were the only animals—it would be such an ugly place. He wondered who had the bees.

Next, he tackled the tools and building materials, which included hammers, mallets, chisels, axes, saws, wrenches, screwdrivers, shovels, hoes, trowels, pitchforks, rakes, spades, awls, pliers, rulers, tape measures, knives, machetes, adzes, pickaxes, levels, hand-planers, wood-files, sharpening stones, nails, screws, bolts, nuts, washers, brushes, synthetic ropes, chains, wires, and a few drills and power tools, which could be powered using one of the portable solar generators. Winthrop had never been much of a handyman because he never needed to be. His life above ground had always been one of wealth and privilege. Whatever needed doing could be paid for. But there was a chest of how-to books with the tools and he spent Tuesdays studying them—Thursdays were spent reading about farming, horticulture, and food processes. There were books on carpentry, woodworking, home building, plumbing, landscaping, water storage and collection, electrical wiring, solar power system construction and maintenance, making mud mortar from scratch, making color pigments and oil paint from scratch, and building and maintaining irrigation and drainage systems. He had neither the raw building materials nor space to practice these new skills, so he'd read each book twice consecutively to ingrain this new knowledge into his head.

There was a stockpile of weapons and ammunition for defense and hunting in a storage locker. Rifles, shotguns, handguns, assault rifles, compound bows and arrows, and an instruction manual on use and maintenance for each weapon. Winthrop had read in the bunker manual that the weapons locker was wired to the rest of the bunker and the mechanical bolt locks on the door would not retract until the locks on the door leading from the bunker to the outside world were deactivated. There was also a variety of fishing rods, reels, spears, nets, tackle, and books on techniques about what rods and lures to use with which fish and how to gut them, along with books on hunting and butchering animals. A separate recreation locker next to the weapons' locker was filled with sporting goods and gear: soccer balls, tennis rackets and balls, a rolled-up net, footballs, basketballs, a hoop and net without a backboard, baseballs, bats, gloves, frisbees, horseshoes, a bocce ball set, a hand pump and needles, binoculars, compasses, three tents and sleeping bags, two hiking backpacks, a deflated inner tube, paddleboards, snorkels, goggles, flippers, arm floaties, water toys, and life vests for children and adults.

Moving forward, he entered the portion of the storage space meant for supplies to be used both in the bunker and after, beginning with a section of the space dedicated to medical supplies and surgical tools with a small library of medical textbooks on diagnosing illnesses, procedures, cures, prenatal care, delivering babies, and books about foraging and harvesting for and making homeopathic cures once supplies ran low above ground. Winthrop's major concern underground was getting enough vitamins and nutrients, of which there were enough to last at least two people for a lifetime.

Winthrop breezed through the clothing and footwear—a wardrobe equipped for four seasons of weather. He only alternated between two sets of the same navy tracksuit, which he cleaned during his weekly shower. After, he'd wring them out and hang them from a clothesline. While they dried, he'd wear his robe or just lounge around naked in sandals.

He checked off all the writing materials and art supplies, then the exercise equipment, which included a series of weights, a few medicine balls, jump ropes, resistance bands, two foam rollers, hand grips, an inflatable stability ball, and an exercise bike that could be rolled anywhere in the bunker. Winthrop had a vast digital library that could be downloaded onto a tablet or read on the workstation screen. But there was a substantial physical library of literature, art, history, philosophy, anthropology, psychology, science, mathematics, and reference books, which the bunker manual described as backup of the great works of human civilization in case the digital archives were ever erased or destroyed. Next to books were board games, a cribbage board, poker chips, and several decks of cards. There was another section for musical instruments, including a guitar, a clarinet, a tenor saxophone, a trumpet, a flute, a violin, an acoustic bass, some hand drums, percussive instruments, a keyboard, several tuning forks, hundreds of backup strings for each of the stringed instruments and hundreds of reeds for the clarinet and saxophone, batteries for the keyboard, books on instruction, and sheet music. All the recorded music was in digital archives, so if it was lost or erased, he would only be able to listen to music he played for himself, which made Winthrop feel obligated to learn how to read music and play as many instruments as possible.

Winthrop finished his inventory counting food stores and hygienic supplies. His entire diet was made up of canned food, dry goods, cooking liquids, and water. There'd been a few jars of honey and pickles, but he went through them all very early, when he was too busy coping with his new life in the bunker to consider conservation tactics. He had an extensive pantry of spices and seasonings to choose from for his meals. When he didn't want to put much thought into it, there were dozens of varieties of flavor powder mix packets to choose from with names like Calcutta Curry, Bangkok Lime, San Juan Pork Roast, and Tuscan Fun. All he had to do was add a mix packet in with a single serving of a starch food, a tablespoon of dehydrated vegetables and a little water, then put it all in the low-liquid power steamer. The available ready-to-cook starches were rice, pasta, oats, cornmeal, creamed wheat, and potato flakes. This offered hundreds of variations of quick meals. If he wanted to cook, there was every variety of flour and grains, butter and dairy powders, sugars, dessert powders, canola oil, soy sauce, rice vinegar, popping corns, dried fruits and fruit skins, canned fishes and seafood, canned beans and vegetables, dried shrimp, meat jerky, nuts, premade granola mixes, and even cannabis powders for some mellow intoxication. There was no liquor of any sort, which was difficult at first. Winthrop had often used alcohol as his first line of self-medication. But, after a couple months, it had stopped occurring to him to want a drink.

He'd shifted a large stash of his personalized daily vitamin packets from the medical and health supply section into the food pantry to remind him to take them every day while choosing his meals. Each packet had twelve pills specially customized for his constitution and medical history to provide all the nutrients he'd need to stay healthy indefinitely underground. He'd counted them all and there were 23,862 daily packets, which would last him just over sixty-five years if need be. Though if he reached twenty-thousand days, he'd start taking them every other day in order to tack on another decade.

After seven hours of taking inventory, Winthrop felt he'd been industrious. He liked having the ninety minutes to wind down and relax before talking to Sophia and Derek. They only talked twice a week. Not knowing how long they would be in the bunkers or how much energy the communications technology used, they erred on the side of conservation. Winthrop used the days between conversations to reflect on what they'd discussed, reminding himself of everything he'd wanted to say but hadn't and any new matters he'd been thinking about since. Sophia and Derek had each other to talk to everyday from morning until night. They could speak gibberish, make small talk, or share comfortable and uncomfortable silences when it fit the mood. But Winthrop had only two hours per week. He couldn't afford to have it taken up with nonsense or quiet. He needed to connect with them to be reminded that social intimacy still existed in the world. The occasional conversation felt forced, usually when Sophia seemed to be having a difficult time. Winthrop would be devastated after. He'd feel awful for days. Worse than after he'd reveled in Ned's loneliness.

Sometimes, when he'd prepared a long list of matters to be discussed, the conversation would last more than an hour. One time, they all talked and debated for nearly four hours. Winthrop was on cloud nine for days following that marathon session. Whenever it fell under an hour, even if it was only by a minute, he'd feel socially inadequate and worthless. To be so painfully boring he couldn't keep their interest for the prescribed sixty minutes, he thought he must be the dullest person underground.

Winthrop wished he was in the same bunker as Sophia. Not to have as a lover, but as a companion. A best friend. Someone to sit next to and comfort. Sexually, Sophia preferred women, which wasn't an issue for Winthrop. Having spent so much time outside of the physical company of another human being, just to have their presence and someone to talk to all the time was enough for him. He had Penelope for sensual gratification, which was simple, uncomplicated, and void of conflict.

He often thought about how hard it must be for Sophia to have started out in a bunker with a living companion who she would never be attracted to. Loneliness and isolation made it easy for Winthrop to shed luxuries like passion and notions of a physical soulmate, but this was not her experience in the bunker. For Sophia, she was being pushed towards a life that was not her own. And what made it even more disturbing was whoever chose and designed the bunkers to put them in, knew everything about them. They knew Sophia's sexual orientation. She had told Winthrop they provided her with a female doll bearing a likeness to her first girlfriend in college, so there was no intention of her suppressing her sexuality. It was explained in each of their personalized bunker life manuals every inhabitant was provided with a companion doll based upon personal tastes and orientations. But the selection process for which inhabitants were partnered in bunkers together had been based entirely upon making reproduction possible, stressing it wasn't about what was right, but what must be. Someone had decided the preservation of humanity and its civilization trumped the individual and their desires.

This issue of species versus individual was a common topic of conversation and debate during their bi-weekly discussions. Winthrop always fell on the side of the individual, arguing civilization was hopeless without free choice. Derek would tell him this was an immature position on the subject, based on privileges irrelevant to survival. The two of them would go back and forth for a while. Sophia always fell in between, sometimes leaning closer to one side or the other, but never fully committing. Winthrop felt deep down she agreed with him, but she had to share a bunker with Derek, so it was wiser not to take sides against her roommate.

Winthrop pedaled on the exercise bike at a casual pace for twenty minutes to work out some of his nervous energy before the video chat, following it up with a series of stretches to relax his body. He drank six ounces of water to hydrate. Supposedly, he had a clean and filtered water supply large enough to sustain two people for a lifetime, but he was skeptical. He couldn't see the artificial reservoir. He only had the information passed along to him in the bunker life manual, which had been written by someone he'd never met. He kept his water intake to sixty ounces per day, which he drank in ten equally staggered installments during his waking hours. After using the bathroom to make sure he wouldn't have to go again for several hours, he sat down at his workstation and placed a video call to Bunker 15B. A soft beeping sound accompanied an appearing and disappearing ellipsis on the screen of his video console to signify the call was attempting to connect. Sophia and Derek appeared before him on the screen.

"Hi, Winthrop," Sophia said, soft-spoken and warmly.

This is how every video chat started. Sophia always spoke first. A simple hello followed by a deep, joyful smile communicating how happy she was to see him. Twice per week, these moments just before the conversation started were the highlight of Winthrop's life. To be reminded another person could be excited to see his face was the difference between being able to comprehend the future and wanting it all to go dark.

"Hi, Sophia," Winthrop said, holding his eyes on her for a moment. "Hi, Derek."

"Hey, Winthrop," Derek said. "I love what you've done with the place."

Derek took the dad-joke approach to coping with the isolated post-apocalypse. His hair was cut very short, almost as if it had been buzzed, but there weren't any hair clippers in the bunkers. Sophia cut it for him. She'd had three younger brothers growing up and one of her household responsibilities was cutting their hair, a skill her grandfather had taught her. When she explained this to Winthrop, she cried. Two of her brothers, twins named Tommy and Don, died in a car accident on the way to their high school prom. The last time she saw them alive they were leaving the house with fresh haircuts. Her brother Tommy had barked, "Smell you later," over his shoulder as he'd closed the door behind him.

Sophia's hair was long, straight, and black. She usually wore it up in a bun during their video chats. She liked wearing cotton tank tops and loose olive-green cargo pants. Derek wore t-shirts and saddle tan-colored work pants. Sometimes he let his red beard grow for a month between trimmings.

They began with the obligatory checklist of questions to find out if anything had changed since their last conversation. *Have you been able to communicate with anyone else underground? Nope. Above ground? Nope. Any readings suggesting the atmosphere up there is getting safer? Nope. Are all of your bunker systems functioning properly? Yes. How's your physical health? Good. Mental well-being? Oh, you know, it's complicated.*

The answers to these questions never changed. According to all their atmospheric monitoring systems, it was still unsafe for them above ground. Not that they could overrule these readings if they wanted to. The doors to the outside could not be opened manually by the inhabitants of the bunkers. The operating system would only deactivate the exterior locks if atmospheric monitors deemed it was safe to go outside or if the oxygen and water systems inside the bunkers failed.

Winthrop wanted to start this conversation on a positive note, even if it was forced. Their last conversation had been sad and intense, which was usually the result of something going on emotionally with Sophia or Winthrop. Derek was the most irreverent of the three and defaulted to joking to get through it all. But the day of their last chat, which had been on Sunday, was his husband Fred's birthday.

"What have you two been watching?" Winthrop asked. "Any good shows I should binge to pass the time? We've…I've been watching a lot of classic movies."

Winthrop would seat Penelope next to him on the couch while he watched movies. He'd put his arm around her and share facts he knew about the making of the films. Once a month, he'd allow himself a bowl of popcorn for a double feature.

"We're between things right now?" Sophia answered. "We

watched a few episodes of *The Little Starchaser* last night. It was my niece Amber's favorite show."

"Any new recipes we should know about?" Derek asked.

"I made burritos," Winthrop answered.

"With what?" Derek responded, dubiously.

"I made tortillas from scratch with flour, baking powder, butter powder, salt, and water," Winthrop said, proudly. "I cooked some seasoned rice and sautéed black beans in a splash of oil with canned tomatoes, San Juan pork powder, avocado powder, Monterey jack powder, sour cream powder, ground coriander, and onion flakes. Then I wrapped it all up in a tortilla with some canned jalapenos. The texture was all wrong, but my taste buds could almost pretend it was a carnitas supreme burrito from Cantina Loco."

"Whatever you say, chef," Derek joked.

"I think it sounds good," Sophia asked. "I miss burritos. Send us the recipe."

"Sure thing."

"Small talk aside," she said, "How are you doing? Really."

"Mostly, I'm okay," Winthrop answered

"What does that mean?" She asked.

"Things could be worse," he said.

"Has the loneliness been hitting you hard this week?"

"Not really," Winthrop said. "I've been thinking about my life outside, just before I ended up here."

"How so?" She asked. Derek was still sitting next to her, but he'd become passive while she questioned Winthrop.

"Sometimes I wish I'd lived differently," Winthrop said. "Less fearful."

"Why?" She asked. "Isn't that the reason you were chosen?"

"I guess," he said, avoiding eye contact with the screen. "What should we call our first city?"

"What?" She asked.

"Or village or whatever," he said. "When we're back above ground, what should we name our first colony?"

"New Bunkertown," Derek said, rejoining the conversation. Winthrop laughed. Sophia smiled and shook her head.

"How would you do things differently in the new colony?" Sophia asked.

"I've never built up a civilization from the ground floor," Winthrop answered. "Everything would be new to me."

"No," she said. "I mean, you said you wish you'd lived differently before the bunker. How would you go about that?"

Winthrop took a moment to think about the question, keeping his gaze away from the camera feed. Even though he knew it wasn't so, whenever he looked straight into the lens, he felt they could see his thoughts like they were reading code.

"I'd try not to obsess so much it drowns out everything else," Winthrop said. He knew he should never have gone after that man. He crossed a line. But he also knew he'd been right about everything. Despite how much his behavior had isolated him from everyone in his life, his predictions were not false byproducts of madness. They were chaotic truths.

Derek asked where New Bunkertown should be, which lightened the mood. Winthrop argued for an inland locale to prepare for the inevitably receding coastline. Derek begged for a beach town. He wanted a view of the ocean, adding that their colonies could move over time and the existing coasts wouldn't be swallowed up in a day. Sophia wanted a home surrounded by trees, big ones. Maybe near a mountain and not so close to everybody else. Despite the isolation of bunker life and how difficult it could be, she still didn't want to be able to see her closest neighbors and vice versa.

Putting geographic preferences aside, they spent the rest of the video call discussing how they would go about establishing a new colony. If it was just the three of them, what would they want their lives to become? Would they even bother with procreating if they were the only survivors? Would they instead only focus on the development and infrastructure necessary to indulge their own fantasies and leisure? Could foregoing the future of humanity pave the way for a long and happy retirement for each of them?

But, if there were others, what then? They made a pact promising the three of them would always stay together and operate as a single unit, protecting and supporting each other against whoever or whatever might be out there. Ideally, anyone else who might be released from bunkers would want to work together to build a new society. But, even with endless resources for researching and vetting candidates, no one could predict the effect such an experience would have on a person. They trusted each other completely but accepted the possibility that psychosis and hate might emerge from other bunkers. Sophia added it was important to think of this only as a worst-case scenario; others would most likely be happy to reunite with more people and work together to build a community.

They ended the call by each offering up something unnecessary they'd want to build in the new world, something selfish. Derek said he'd want a tennis court. Sophia said an art studio, explaining she'd always loved painting and drawing and sculpture, but had never made much time for it. She'd never felt, as an adult, it was practical enough to fully embrace. Winthrop wasn't sure, maybe a study with bookshelves, a writing desk, and a comfortable reading chair. All he could imagine wanting to do outside the bunker was going on nature walks. Writing in a journal about what plants and animals he saw. Birdwatching. Camping with friends. Just having friends to be out in the world with. Enjoying a slower and less urban pace than he had before.

After they signed off, Winthrop thought about the other potential survivors and if they were out there, how far away they were. His was only one bunker away from 15B if they were situated in some sort of alphanumerical order. Winthrop wished they'd built tunnels connecting the bunkers. It would have changed everything underground. They could have had a real community. He understood the big-picture benefits of compartmentalizing the survivors. If any of them had been infected with a contagious virus or bacteria when they entered their bunker, it would likely spread to everyone they had access to. He wondered if all the bunkers were designed to accommodate two people or if they varied in size. Had families been allowed to stay together?

These were brief contemplations. He was wiped out. The letdown just after a video chat colliding with the nervous adrenaline he'd felt all day leading up to their conversation was always rough and he'd have low energy for the rest of the day. He walked over to the lounge space and let himself fall into the sofa, sinking as far as the cushions would allow.

The osprey soared across the wall screen, swerving away from the tree line and diving back down towards the lake and breaking through the water's surface. This time it lifted off with a smallmouth bass in its talons. The raptor soon disappeared into the horizon as its meal still struggled to break free.

Winthrop decided it was a double feature night and thought about what they should watch, narrowing his field down to a classic noir followed by a comedy—maybe a Humphrey Bogart and Cary Grant to highlight two of his favorites. He went to his bedroom to retrieve Penelope and make her comfortable on the sofa before he made popcorn.

PART TWO: THE HOLT INSTITUTE

Sophia stood up from her chair facing the video console and reached her hands towards the ceiling in a stretch. Derek had already left the video-chat room. She took a moment and then walked out into a larger room, closing the door behind her and grabbing a white lab coat off a hook on the wall. She wasn't required to wear a coat, but it made her feel more professional until she had an opportunity to change out of the tank top and cargo pants. One wall was mounted with video monitors displaying views of every inch of Bunker 15C from multiple angles. On one screen, Winthrop was in the kitchen-ette placing a bowl full of popcorn onto a tray with salt and pepper shakers. He mixed a flavor powder into a glass of water and set it next to the bowl, picked up the tray and left the room. "18 months 2 weeks 5 days" was written at the top of a large whiteboard on the wall opposite the video monitors.

Derek was sitting at one end of a long table, typing up a report of their video session with Winthrop. The space was an open plan with a long table, two sitting desks, four standing desks, a long wall of monitors, and a long wall of whiteboards. Anjali, their senior lab technician, was checking the levels on all of Winthrop's vitals. The video chats could be stressful and emotionally jarring to him, so they found it important to make sure there were no physiological spikes or drops directly after the chat. Since this had been a relatively positive and mild-tempered conversation, checking his vitals was a matter of following procedure. There was no real concern over the results and what they might render.

Winthrop appeared on the monitor offering the research team a straight view of the couch from the perspective of the viewing screen. He set the tray of popcorn and his drink on the coffee table and sat next to Penelope, putting his arm around her and kissing her gently on the cheek. He told her he thought they'd start with a Bogart noir and then move on to something lighter with Cary Grant, maybe *Bringing Up Baby* or *Charade*, adding it all depended on which Hepburn he was in the mood for after they finished the Bogart film, Katherine or Audrey. His smirk showed self-amusement with the Hepburn joke. He'd chosen *Dark Passage* to start and explained to her while it's not as well-known as some of the other Bogart and Bacall noirs, the movie begins from the camera's first-person perspective and Bogart is not seen until after his character heals from reconstructive facial surgery and removes the bandages.

"I've always thought it was such a fascinating stylistic choice by the director," Winthrop said. "You never see the character's original face. Bogart is the reconstruction."

Sophia turned down the volume on the sound accompanying the monitors once the movie began. Winthrop often talked at length about the films to introduce them, but once a film began, he wouldn't utter a word until it was over. It was nearly 7pm, which was late to be in the lab, but they typically worked longer hours on the days of the video chats because there was at least an hour of work to be done after the chat: typing up the session report on the video chat, checking the vitals, and making sure all of the environmental and technical systems in the Bunker 15C Habitat were functioning normally for the night. The next afternoon, the three of them would have a meeting to discuss the video chat and any observations they made about Winthrop's progress or regression. Then, they would formulate a work plan for the days leading up to the next video chat and begin planning their approach. Should the next session be pleasant and amiable? Should they fabricate tension between Sophia and Derek, or create a personal trauma to set the mood? How long should the session be? Much of this would be decided by the nature and results of the last few chats preceding it. Winthrop's current emotional and mental state was another major factor in designing the next session. Additionally, they'd all agreed early on that if every chat was happy and ended positively, Winthrop might suspect there was something off about his entire bunker existence. Tension and awkwardness were natural, especially under dire or tragic circumstances.

While they finished up for the evening, Andrei showed up for the nightshift. He was one of three lab techs working directly under Anjali who took turns monitoring the Bunker 15C Habitat throughout the night. At the long table facing the video monitors, he set up his work nest, which consisted of a laptop, a 32-ounce travel cup of iced coffee, and a pile of snacks. Of all the lab techs, Andrei was the most hard-wired for nocturnal solitude. He was pale and full of quiet energy, listening to books and podcasts as he worked. Sometimes he barely noticed them during the turnover to the nightshift. He'd grunt hello as he began to review the daily reports and check the levels and status of the habitat's systems. Anjali would ask a few random questions like "What's your favorite color?" or "Why are my shoes always on fire?" to make sure Andrei was paying attention and hadn't put his mind on autopilot all night, but he always answered all of her questions accurately and literally, no matter how ludicrous they were. He had a mind for multitasking, but not sarcasm.

Sophia, Derek, and Anjali all walked out of the building together. A large metal sign attached to a monolithic concrete slab near the main entrance of the building read: The Holt Institute for Behavioral & Habitat Research. Derek and Anjali waited at the company shuttle stop together, which would drop them both near their homes in New Bedford, but Sophia walked towards her car in the parking lot. She lived with her wife Kelly in Providence, which was not on the shuttle's route. She didn't mind the commute. New Bedford felt like an extension of the company, an annex. Not for any reason but its proximity. If they lived close by, she worried it'd be too easy to stay later in the lab every day or go in on the weekends. Maintaining a healthy separation between church and state wasn't intuitive for her, she was a natural workhorse and needed the physical distance.

Sophia sat in her car for five minutes to decompress and collect herself. The days of video chats with Winthrop were becoming more taxing on her, and since these were also the days she worked the latest, she didn't want to bring the lab home with her for what little time she and Kelly would have together before they went to bed. She practiced some deep breathing exercises and thought about what music she wanted to play to help her relax during the drive home.

She watched the shuttle pick up Derek and Anjali, then started her car and left the parking lot. The company property covered a large stretch of land and it was a three-minute drive to the front gates from her building. When she reached the campus exit, she stopped at one of the security booths. The guard said hello and asked if she was taking any company property off campus for the night. She answered no except for maybe herself. He laughed at her joke while he looked into her car, raised the boom gate, and waved her on.

Sophia drove away. To the left of the front gate in seven-foot letters attached to the twelve-foot concrete perimeter wall, illuminated by ground-level spotlights, was the company name: Phyla.

The drive home was about forty minutes and she usually opted for music that was soothing to her—not necessarily quiet or mellow, but something personally comforting, sentimental. She chose Ben Webster for the night's commute. She loved the tenor saxophone and his subtones on ballads always eased her nerves.

Lately, Sophia had been thinking a lot about her decision to leave an academic career to take over the Holt Institute. When she made the decision, she'd only focused on the opportunities this career shift would provide for her work—more funding than she could ever dream of, and complete autonomy to run any research or projects she was inspired by.

Staring at the road in front of her, she thought about the first phone call she had ever received from Alistair Holt.

———————

Initially, she hadn't believed it was really Holt and had told him so. She'd have thought one of his personal assistants would make all his phone calls for him. It was a poorly executed prank. He laughed and hung up. Ten seconds later she received a video call from him and immediately apologized for her behavior.

"Nonsense," he'd said. "I don't want any apologies for honesty. I'm not nearly as formal as my net worth might suggest."

She nodded her head and said nothing. She was waiting for a question and studying him on the screen. As many times as she'd seen his photo or watched him in an interview, it felt different watching him speak directly to her. If the conversation had been in person, she'd have had the urge to stick him with the tip of a pin to make sure he was real and in the flesh. He looked good for his age, which fell somewhere in the mid-to-late sixties, but she couldn't remember exactly how old he was. His well-trimmed salt-and-pepper beard had been salt-and-pepper for at least fifteen years in the public eye. He had a warm and welcoming persona. He was so much more approachable than she'd imagined. It was hard not to like him and want him to like you back.

"Not much of a talker, are you?" he said. "Well, I think it's safe to assume you know all about me, but this call is about you."

"Why do you know about me?" Sophia asked.

"You're quite impressive," he said. "Two years into your first academic professorship and you're a shoo-in for tenure. It's a foregone conclusion. Your research on the psychological effects of the physical environment and the therapeutic qualities of one's habitat are, in a word, brilliant."

"Thank you," she'd said while trying to temper her nausea.

"I'd like you to come visit me at Phyla so we can talk about your future."

"What are you proposing?" she'd asked.

"You're on the path to a long and successful career," he said. "There's no denying it, but I'd like you to consider taking a position as Director of a new behavioral institute at Phyla."

"What kind of projects would I be working on?" Sophia asked.

"I'd rather discuss it in person," he said. "We can send a car to pick you up in Boston."

"When?" she responded.

"Can you clear your schedule for tomorrow?" he asked.

Sophia remembered running to the bathroom after the call and throwing up. The same thing happened when she was offered the position as assistant professor. Exhilaration and anticipatory fear unsettled her stomach. Since high school, she'd always tried to isolate herself at home while waiting to hear back about important news. During her senior year, after she'd submitted the last of her college applications, she unsuccessfully attempted to convince her parents she'd contracted mono and would have to stay home for weeks, maybe even months.

A growl from Webster's tenor brought her out of the memory. She was only about ten minutes from home. They lived in a four-bedroom Victorian. It needed a little updating, but the bones were good and everything was in working order. It was the kind of house they'd fantasized about since they first moved into an apartment together nearly a decade earlier. A house they would never have been able to afford in Boston on her professor's salary. Kelly had been working on the house full-time since they'd moved in, which was fine with Sophia. As much time as she spent thinking about and conceptualizing habitats and occupied spaces, she had no interest in carpentry or any home renovation projects. She preferred enjoying the fruits of her wife's labor.

Kelly loved fixing up the house, and ever since she found out she was pregnant a month earlier, she'd been working double-time to have the house ready for the baby. She'd redesigned the kitchen, making it the only completely contemporary room in the house, and removed the non-load-bearing wall between the kitchen and the family room to create an open common space. She also built a large back deck where there had been steps out the French doors, which opened out from the family room onto the yard. These were the only major projects. The rest of the work involved minor updates to appliances and bathrooms. When all of this was completed, the rooms would be redecorated. Kelly planned to have the house finished by the time she was six months pregnant and she was on schedule to reach this goal.

They had met in college. They were both enrolled in the same oil-painting class. Sophia was a senior and Kelly was a junior. It took a little while before they spoke to each other directly. Sophia was uneasy taking an art class. She was focused on her thesis research in psychology and after that most of her energy was spent compiling materials for internship and graduate school applications. She felt irresponsible taking a painting class, but secretly cherished it. This insistence on approaching everything with such rigid seriousness didn't come from her family. Her parents were very accomplished in their own careers—a neurosurgeon and a professor of American History—but encouraged Sophia to make time for her own enjoyment, so they were thrilled when they found out she'd enrolled in the painting class. She'd told them she needed it to fulfill a studio art requirement to graduate, but they knew this was not true.

Kelly was more at home in the art studio. She had two majors and two minors and was always trying to decide which she was going to drop in order to graduate on time.

Sophia presented herself as a fish out of water in class, but Kelly observed the hidden joy on Sophia's face every time they started painting. Sophia would complain, but the moment they sat at their easels and started working on a still life, she was lost to the outside world and wouldn't utter a word or look away until it was time to leave.

"You pretend like you don't," Kelly said to her one day when they were cleaning their brushes in the sink, "but you love this class more than any of us."

Sophia didn't respond. She focused on her fingers rubbing oil soap into the bristles of one of her brushes.

"I think it's ready to rinse," Kelly said with a smile. She found Sophia's reticence endearing.

Sophia stopped what she was doing and rinsed the bristles.

"Don't worry, your secret is safe with me," she said, handing Sophia a piece of paper with her phone number written on it and walked away.

Ten months later, they moved into a one-bedroom apartment together. Sophia was beginning a research internship, which would be followed by graduate school. Kelly was in her senior year and had no idea what she was going to do after. Something with her hands, she'd say, like horticulture or woodworking, or maybe teaching or law school. Sophia would make a joke about the use of hands in law school to hide how stressful Kelly's lack of a life-plan was for her.

When Sophia walked into their house, Kelly had a dinner spread waiting for her on the coffee table in the family room. She'd made hummus and a tomato, cucumber, and feta salad with olive oil and fresh oregano. A plate of grilled pita and a bottle of chilled vinho verde rounded out the meal. They sat next to each other on their linen sofa, a gray mid-century modern reproduction, and talked about their days. Kelly put in a new toilet in the downstairs bathroom and started comparing paint samples on the walls of their bedroom.

"I'm leaning towards the porcelain blue eggshell," Kelly said, dipping a piece of pita in the hummus. "But I could be persuaded otherwise. How was your day?"

"It was fine," Sophia said. "And I liked that color when we looked at all the swatches. Just nothing yellowish."

"I was thinking of using the squash blossom yellow matte we looked at for the kitchen," Kelly said. "It reminds me of the Sun."

"It reminds me of pee," Sophia responded, which got them both laughing.

"Maybe for the bathroom then," Kelly joked. "How was the video chat?"

Sophia wanted to gloss over the subject and offer her wife an answer less impersonal but equivalent to saying that *all progress is two steps forward and one step back. Boring but boring is a good thing sometimes. Any forward motion is a victory. This is a long game and we're still in the first inning/quarter/period/half/lane/lap/hole. Human behavior is a lot like painting interiors in a house: you don't just throw paint at the wall; you have to choose colors and finishes; drop cloths have to be placed underneath and windows taped wherever the frame meets glass; a primer has to be rolled on before the first and maybe second coat if it's an old house with a long history of inhabitants; different rooms might need different colors and finishes; then you have to let it dry and see how it looks to make sure you chose the right paint and applied it correctly and don't have to start over again with a whole new approach to hues and techniques.*

"I like him," Sophia answered.

"Who?" Kelly asked, confused and a little worried.

"Winthrop."

"What do you mean you like him?" Kelly asked. She filled Sophia's glass with wine.

"Not *like* like," Sophia answered. "I mean I'm beginning to care about him as a friend. A good friend. I've developed a strong affection for him."

"I know," Kelly said. "Does that complicate the work?"

"It does," Sophia said, nodding. "I've been feeling guilty about what we're doing with him. To him."

"Has something changed?" Kelly asked.

"When I first started feeling this way, I thought maybe I'd been so caught up in the opportunity to run my own research institute and just hadn't really put enough thought into the reality that this project could go on for years or even decades," Sophia said. "But, if I'm really being honest with myself, I didn't think I'd ever actually grow to like him."

"What are you going to do?"

"I don't think I can do this for several years," Sophia said.

"Well, I'm sure you'd have your choice of universities," Kelly said. Her blind confidence that everything would work out for them allowed Kelly to be unconditionally supportive of any life decisions Sophia made. If the tables were turned, Sophia would be having a panic attack, which would only be amplified by her fear of how the panic attack could impact the pregnancy.

"I'm not sure Alistair Holt will write me any glowing job references if I jump ship without much advanced warning," Sophia said. "It's his son. Any exit will have to leave the project in the hands of someone he approves of. If not, he could make me a pariah on the academic job market. Or any job market for that matter."

"We'll figure this out," Kelly said. "He can't expect you to stay there forever."

"I think he can," Sophia said, washing down an oil-soaked chunk of feta with some wine. She scooped up a dollop of hummus with a triangle of pita, spooned some tomato and cucumber on top, and stuffed the whole thing in her mouth. It took her fifteen seconds or so before she could chew up and swallow enough to take another sip of her wine to make way for talking. She didn't share with Kelly her other conflicted feelings about leaving the job.

She wasn't only worried about the punitive consequences of leaving. Holt's approval meant a lot to her. Despite the ways in which their relationship was complicated, she thought of him as a mentor with a little splash of grandfather mixed in. He was eccentric, which could be very awkward at times, occasionally to the degree she was angry with herself for feeling any fondness for him. But she still didn't want to disappoint him. No one outside of her family and Kelly had ever shown so much faith in her potential and what she could accomplish.

"What colors are you considering for the nursery?" Sophia asked.

"What are your thoughts on sage green?"

"Don't get me started on sage green," Sophia said, finishing her wine and tilting her glass for more.

Kelly made them bacon, egg, and cheese sandwiches on scallion biscuits the next morning. Sophia went to the Institute later on Thursdays. After working late on Wednesdays, she needed some time at home to have a leisurely breakfast with Kelly, do the crossword together, or read a novel or magazine. She tried to relax and embrace the slow morning. But her anxieties about work and Winthrop overwhelmed her thoughts, so she requested a morning of quiet reading. She believed this was a clever way to hide her stress, but Kelly knew Sophia wasn't in a great place whenever she insisted they quietly read on a Thursday morning. It was one of Sophia's many tells.

Sophia left for work at 9:30am. The traffic was heavy, which meant the commute would last at least an hour. Her car windows were heavily tinted to block sunlight. She listened to the end of a morning news show she liked and then put on some Alice Coltrane. The music didn't necessarily take her to a happier place but created a more comforting landscape for her anxieties. She felt it was like having one of her best friends drive her to the hospital to have her appendix removed. It didn't erase the destination, but it made her feel loved.

––––––––––––

Sophia recalled her first visit to Phyla's headquarters on the outskirts of New Bedford. She'd sat alone in the backseat of the luxury SUV, which had picked her up at her apartment building in Boston. The seats were some sort of soft leather, probably harvested clone hide and more comfortable than any piece of furniture she'd ever sat on. They passed through the security gates without stopping and drove directly to the executive complex, which contained Alistair Holt's offices, several conference rooms, a restaurant, a personal gym, and a suite with a bedroom, lounge, and bathroom for Holt to stay in when he didn't feel like going home.

Holt was waiting for her on the front steps of the building wearing a denim shirt and brown canvas pants, which both looked as though they'd never been worn before. He walked over to her and put his hand out. He had a good handshake. He didn't squeeze like he was showing her how much stronger his grip was than all of the other powerful men in the world. It was friendly, but not soft and creepy. The anticipation of a first handshake made Sophia uncomfortable. In her experience, handshakes didn't bring out the best in people. They were private exchanges where true intentions were whispered through squeezes. She loathed them.

"How would you like a tour of the grounds?" He asked, gesturing to an army green jeep with its top removed. "We can discuss the job offer and you can see what we do here, up close."

"I'd like that," she said. One of Holt's attorneys presented her with a non-disclosure agreement to sign before she got into the vehicle.

The jeep took a single-lane road wending its way through a series of fenced-off areas and enclosures. There was a gray rectangular building to the left with a small sign, which read: Project Astronaut. A massive pack of young black dogs ran around the field adjacent to the building. They all looked the same, identical aside from some variation in ages. Their ears were pointed and snouts lupine but overall looked more like a mix of husky and German Shepherd than wolf.

"My latest project," Holt said, pointing at the dogs. "Hush hush."

The dogs ran to the section of fence nearest the jeep, yelping as they slowly drove by. There were at least a hundred of them.

The fences were taller for the next series of habitats, each housing a different species and spacious enough for the animals to run around—more like a safari park than a city zoo. Sophia could see giraffes, zebras, elk, moose, kudus, goats, and wildebeests. She could tell there were more enclosures out of sight behind those bordering the road, though she couldn't guess how many or how deep they went. She heard an elephant's trumpet but couldn't see the animal.

"We separate our herbivore enclosures from our carnivore enclosures," Holt said. "We've found it calms their collective behaviors if there's some distance between them. It's a facilities protocol inspired by a talk I heard you give, which was titled, 'Your Habitat is Your Universe.'"

"How many different species do you have here?" Sophia asked.

"So many," Holt answered. "If you accept my job offer, you'll see them all."

The jeep drove away from the herbivores. A half-mile down the road, they passed through the entrance to the carnivore territory. On the left side of the road were feline enclosures including

African lions, jaguars, leopards, snow leopards, clouded leopards, mountain lions, Bengal tigers, Siberian tigers, and Indochinese tigers. The right side of the road was lined with canine enclosures for gray wolves, maned wolves, red foxes, African wild dogs, dholes, coyotes, and black-backed jackals.

"There are many more species of felines, canines, and other mammalian carnivores, which can't be seen from the road," Holt said. "And all of the non-mammalian carnivores and herbivores are housed in different areas of the property, which we won't see on our ride today—except for the birds."

"This is all exciting and very impressive," Sophia said as she stared at a jaguar, pacing side-to-side along the bars of its enclosure and staring back at her. "When are you going to tell me about the job?"

"All business," Holt responded. "Not the worst quality in a potential collaborator. Let's get out and stroll for a bit."

The jeep came to a stop. Sophia and Holt got out and walked down the center of the road. The jeep crept slowly behind, always leaving at least ten yards between them. They left the carnivore territory and entered a stretch of road with meadows on either side. In the near distance, Sophia could see buildings a quarter mile to her right and some sort of tall perimeter wall a little further in the opposite direction. She wanted to ask how much land Phyla occupied. It was much vaster than she'd imagined. But she didn't want to distract Holt away from the subject matter at hand, which he'd been taking his time to broach as if he were trying to charm her into agreeing to something without offering any details first.

"I would like you to be director of the soon to be established Holt Institute for Behavioral & Habitat Research," he said.

"Exactly what kind of research would I be director of?" She

asked. "While I'm interested in studying the behavior and habitats of animals, the subjects of my research are exclusively human. Are you going to start cloning people too?"

"Good god no," Holt responded with a deep guttural laugh. "I have no interest in that can of worms. Even though it would be housed on this property, this institute wouldn't be directly related to the work of Phyla."

"What would it be then?" She asked.

"Whatever you make of it," he said. "Your ideas have been inspiring to my work and the ways in which I approach my everyday life. I want to offer you the opportunity to explore your research without constraint. Unfettered. Whenever you have an idea for a new research project, you won't need my permission to pursue it."

"Why are you offering this to me?" She asked. "And don't say it's just because you felt inspired by one of my lectures a year ago."

Sophia was overcome with nausea and begged her own belly not to vomit all over her potential employer.

"You're not going to make this easy for me," he said, stopping in the middle of the road and raising his arm to signal the jeep behind them. "And I like it. I don't make it a practice to surround myself with weak-minded souls. Never have, and I truly believe it's one of the secrets to my success."

He looked around at the meadows as he searched for his words. A lion roared, causing a trickle of anxious calls and responses from other animals in the distance.

"There would be one research project you'd be required to carry out," he said. "You'd be free to direct any other projects simultaneously—but getting this project up and running would be a priority."

"And what is the nature of this project?" Sophia asked, unenthusiastically.

"Your ideas about the use of habitat in designing therapeutic processes is at the heart of this project," Holt said with a rising intensity. "That's why I chose you."

The way he said the word "chose" made Sophia realize this proposition of employment had never been hers to say no to. The tone of his voice made her feel as though she'd already signed a binding contract.

He noticed her hesitation. How she recoiled and looked over to the jeep. How she reached into the pants pocket where she'd put her phone away. How she was searching for her tools of escape.

"It's my son," he said, gentler and more vulnerable. "Winthrop."

"Your son?" she asked.

"He would be the subject," he said. "He's always been a good boy mind you, but the world has been challenging for him, and there's been an incident."

Sophia didn't respond. She looked him in the eyes and waited.

"He hurt someone," Holt said, looking down at his feet.

"Hurt?" She asked.

"He attacked someone," he said. "You see, Winthrop is afraid of the world. Of what he's convinced is coming. And, sometimes, he lashes out."

"What does he think is coming?" she asked with less reluctance in her voice. She was curious about people. It was her nature.

"Everything," he said earnestly. "Chemical weapons. Biological weapons. Nuclear attacks. Global warfare. A secular end of days."

"And why did he attack someone?"

"He was scared," Holt said. "He'll see someone at a shopping mall or at a restaurant behave in a way that seems out of the ordinary and it sets him off."

"Did he kill someone?" Sophia asked.

"No…no," Holt said. "But these episodes often occur in public places, and this time was worse than the others. It's the first time he was violent against another person and it's only a matter of time before he does something my resources and influence won't be able to fix."

"What am I doing here?" Sophia asked.

Holt started walking down the road away from the jeep.

"What if we fabricated what he believes to be reality?" Holt said, walking ahead of her. "What if we create a universe for him? One where he feels safe?"

"For how long?" She asked.

"I don't know," he said.

They walked past a road leading to a ten-foot-high perimeter wall with a large, gated entrance. A metal sign was staked in the ground on the side of the road leading up to the gate. It read: "Old Dartmouth. No Trespassing!" Before she could ask what was behind the wall, he told her it was off limits to all employees of Phyla, then pointed up ahead. A massive aviary rose from behind a small hill where the road disappeared. The sounds of what she imagined to be hundreds of different species of birds drowned out the wind and the jeep's slow-moving engine as they got closer.

———————

When Sophia entered the Institute, it was 10:45am. Derek and Anjali were sitting at the long table, ready to discuss the previous day's video chat with Winthrop. It was early for a meeting, but they were both situated with all of their wares: notebooks, pens, digital tablets, printouts, baked goods, and coffee. Derek was usually the laid-back member of the team, but his body language was anxious and impatient. He was shifting in his seat every half-second or so.

"Why so eager this morning?" Sophia asked. "We usually don't get started until after lunch on Thursdays."

"Seriously?" Derek said, shaking his head. "Fred and I have a meeting with the adoption agency today. It's at 1pm and we were supposed to start this meeting forty-five minutes ago. It's been on the schedule for weeks."

"I'm so sorry, Derek" Sophia said. "It slipped my mind. We can have a brief meeting right now so I'll have something to report to Mr. Holt when I meet with him later this afternoon, then we can meet again tomorrow to discuss anything else we want to address about yesterday's video chat."

"Fine," Derek said. "But I need to leave in half an hour. Fred and I are meeting up for lunch to prepare. We're trying to adopt an infant with at least a partial educational voucher attached to them. Do you have any idea how much competition there is for those children? We'll be going against families with more resources than we have, so we need them to like us a lot. We need to make them love us."

Sophia stopped herself from saying it would all work out, and let the meeting begin. Anjali quickly went over all of Winthrop's vitals, both during the video chat and the hours following. All his readings were relatively stable, suggesting he was in a positive mood at the end of the chat. But he wasn't ecstatic, so the descent in his mood from social interaction to solitude was not a drastic high to low drop. Anjali had observed this seemed to be Winthrop's sweet spot. If he was over-excited and joyous at the end of a chat, the following days would devolve into a deep depression. At the other end of the spectrum, when the meeting didn't go well or ended in a sad place, he'd be moderately depressed until the next chat, but the pressure he felt to make it better the next time they talked would bring on an acute rise in his stress levels. Both extremes resulted in a more aggressive regime of medication under Derek's supervision, which always made Alistair Holt unhappy. He did not want Winthrop living in a state of medicated solitude. The purpose of the institute was to avoid that approach.

With these findings from Anjali's analysis, Sophia would attempt to create a habitat and mood in Bunker 15C conducive to containing Winthrop's responses and actions within these emotional extremes. This last chat marked four weeks without having to increase Winthrop's dosages. It was a milestone.

"I think we're getting the hang of this," Anjali said. "Mr. Holt will be very pleased with our progress controlling the habitat."

"I agree," Derek said. "And I think if we're able to maintain this for another four weeks, we should try lowering his baseline dosages of medication. But we should wait a couple weeks before we present this to Holt."

Sophia watched Winthrop on one of the monitor screens. He was in the large common space, doing a series of strengthening exercises with dumbbells while he watched an episode of *The Little Starchaser*. It wasn't the type of show he preferred watching, but after a video chat, he would always watch, read, or listen to the movies, television shows, books, and music Sophia mentioned during their conversation. Of all the things, watching him do this because she had brought it up made Sophia feel ashamed for invading his privacy. Even more than when the monitors showed him having sex with Penelope.

"Sophia," Derek said. "What do you think?"

She looked over to her colleagues and took a moment to remind herself what they were discussing.

"He's getting better," Sophia said.

"That's what we've been saying," Anjali said.

"But what are we going to do?" Sophia asked.

"About what?" Derek asked. "Why do you seem so disappointed?"

"What do we do if he gets significantly better?" Sophia asked. "Are we going to leave him there?"

"All of the progress we've made would implode on itself if he learned this entire habitat was fabricated and the outside world was safe to live in," Anjali said. "He can't ever leave."

"How do we know it's a success if we can't observe the subject after the treatment is completed?" Sophia asked.

"We don't," Anjali answered. "Not for sure, which is why our next subject should be treated under less extreme circumstances. We're following orders with Winthrop, which will provide us with the resources we'll need to attempt this treatment on *our* terms without interference. Ideally, the next subject won't be placed in an environment that shuts them off from access to what is happening in the outside world. It will need to be a smaller fabrication. One that allows the possibility of reentering society."

"You're acting strange, Sophia," Derek said, "and I don't have time to start unpacking whatever's going on with you. I have to go meet Fred."

Derek gathered his things and left.

"He's right," Anjali said. "Is everything okay at home?"

"Yeah," Sophia answered. "It's probably just exhaustion. Between this project, sketching out plans for new research initiatives, and getting the house ready for the baby, I think I'm wearing myself thin."

Sophia desperately wanted to share how she was feeling about Winthrop with someone she worked with. She trusted her colleagues so long as they were on the same broad page, but if she admitted to having reservations about the Bunker 15C project as a whole, she worried they'd feel betrayed by her and, ultimately, their loyalties would be to their own careers.

"You should take a few days off," Anjali said. "You haven't taken more than one consecutive day off since this project began. That's not good."

"With two video chats with Winthrop each week and all of the necessary preparation," Sophia said, "I can't possibly take more than a day off."

"Yes, you can," Anjali insisted. "Derek took almost a whole week off once. I think you said he had a bad reaction to one of the flavor packets and wasn't feeling up for the chat. Winthrop didn't question it and we found no negative change in his mood in the days following Derek's absence."

"I remember," Sophia responded. "It caused us to consider his moods might be more significantly affected by the ways in which he perceives we respond to him than the amount of time he spends chatting with us. If Winthrop had felt Derek skipped a chat because of him, it would have been devastating, but an absence due to peripheral circumstances was not enough to provoke anxiety or depression."

"Right," Anjali said. "So, get a fake migraine and go spend a week relaxing at home with Kelly before the baby comes—because if you think preparing the house for the baby is exhausting, you're about to enter a world of hurt."

Sophia chuckled and nodded to communicate she was in agreement. Anjali had two young children of her own, a son and daughter, aged two and four. She made a lot of jokes about the difficulties of parenthood. They often involved the many joys of alcohol or finding an escape hatch. Sophia always laughed, but she didn't like these jokes. The challenges of balancing her own professional ambitions while trying to be a good partner and hopefully soon a good parent were already very difficult for Sophia. She wanted to be surrounded by people who were positive about parenthood. She wanted them to fill her mind with anecdotes reaffirming why it's a good idea to have children.

"I'm off to grab lunch at the café and eat outside," Anjali said, standing up from the table. "I could eat inside if you care to join?"

"No," Sophia said. "I'm going to go over some things and then prepare for my meeting with Mr. Holt later. Thanks for your advice, I think I do need a vacation, even if it's at home in Providence."

Sophia opened her laptop to outline some notes to prepare for her meeting with Holt. They met one-on-one a day or two after every video chat with Winthrop. She would recount the details of the video chat, which she thought was redundant knowing Holt watched the recording of every session. Then she would discuss their observations about the chat and any changes or plans they had for the project moving forward. The meetings were mostly dull. They occurred so frequently, Sophia struggled to find new things to report, which meant rephrasing thoughts she'd already shared with him. Despite the regurgitated information, Holt always seemed happy with her updates.

The first time she ever met with Holt to discuss Winthrop's progress was awkward. Up until then, Sophia had felt relatively comfortable when she was around him.

She'd never seen his office and the décor was overwhelming. The room was filled with objects of Colonial New England, which she assumed were almost entirely reproductions because of their condition, not because he couldn't afford the real thing. They all looked so new, and they were everywhere. Kitchen utensils, tools, weapons, outfits, quills, and furs. There was a display case of wampum.

And bison. A lot of bison. Paintings. Figurines. Tapestries. Photographs. They were his favorite animal. Even though New England wouldn't have been their stomping ground, he had an infatuation with them rivaling his obsession with the region's history.

Walking into his office was like looking deep inside of Holt, as if Sophia had walked in through his chest cavity and took the express elevator straight up to his innermost thoughts and feelings. There was nothing inside of the room suggesting a connection to Phyla or cloning or any of his professional achievements, which were many. There were no award plaques or framed university degrees on the walls. She also found it strange none of the objects in his office or the era they represented were reflected in any of the designs or decorations throughout the rest of the company's buildings or properties. These collectibles were personal to him, and very few people had seen the inside of his office. Most of his meetings were held in one of the conference rooms.

Holt gestured for her to sit in the wooden chair facing him. The seat was historically authentic but much less comfortable than the soft leather seats in the company SUV.

"How are you?" Holt asked. "Are you feeling settled in here? Do you have everything you need at the Institute?"

"Yes," she answered. "The facilities are incredible. Thank you."

"This project is a priority," he said. "So, if there's anything needed, please let me know."

Sophia was distracted by the room. When she sat down, she looked around and took mental notes of everything she saw, ending at the wampum display and studying it for several moments.

"You're Wampanoag, right?" Holt asked.

"I am," she responded, defensive. "How is that relevant?"

"You don't talk about it much, do you?"

"I don't *not* talk about it," she said. "But it doesn't really come up in the laboratory. What's your interest in my ethnic background?"

"Nothing of consequence," he answered. "But, as you can see, I'm a student and enthusiast of early New England and the region."

"Oh," she said, trying to hold back the disappointment in her tone while still communicating she didn't want this to become a recurring topic of conversation between them. "I wasn't around back then."

Holt laughed loudly and gave himself a moment before he continued.

"I came across an old journal from the early 1670s, before King Philip's War, written by a settler who was documenting the whole process of building his saltbox colonial house," he said. "There were other observations on the land and your people, local incidents between colonists he'd witnessed, the weather, flora and fauna."

"Sounds fascinating," Sophia said.

"I had a saltbox colonial house built using his journal to create an exact replica," he said with enthusiasm. She'd never seen him so excited about anything. "My architects and contractors did an exquisite job. It was just as I had pictured it in my head when I was reading the journal. It was as if they'd accessed my imagination."

"What does this all have to do with me?" Sophia asked.

"It's about habitats and recreating them," he said. "And it's intertwined with the history of your people. I saw you looking at the wampum."

"As much as I love my family," Sophia interjected, "I'm not here to discuss them. I'm here to talk about your son."

"Of course," he said. "My apologies for any insensitivity. I get excited and carried away, but I'm overstepping. How is Winthrop?"

"He's accepted the scenario we've fabricated for him," she said. "But it's still too early to know whether the impact it has on him is positive or negative in relation to his prior emotional and mental health. We've only just started."

"But he believes the scenario is real?" Holt asked, looking not at Sophia but at his collectibles.

"Yes," she responded. "He thinks the bunker is real."

"Good."

PART THREE: THE BISON IN THE LABORATORY

Winthrop undressed Penelope in the bedroom. She'd been wearing a sporty fitted black pullover dress with fishnet stockings—an outfit her character Warbird would have worn with leather combat boots and a denim jacket riddled with buttons and iron-on patches. As he began to take his own clothes off, Sophia stood up from the long table and turned away from the monitors, telling Derek she needed some fresh air. He reminded her to cover up.

Another drawback to the project was the need to appear as if they hadn't been outside in over eighteen months. Sophia missed exposing her skin to the sun, feeling the warmth of it being absorbed through her pores. She missed being a sponge for its light. She missed beaches and swimming outdoors during the day, and often thought about what it would mean for her physical health and happiness if this project went on for years or even decades, which was looking more likely as the months accumulated. Winthrop was in good health and followed all the steps necessary to maintain it. He took all his vitamins, exercised daily, and ate as healthy as he could on a diet without fresh or perishable foods. He could survive for decades in the bunker following this regimen, plus the medications and nutrients they administered to him when they put him under while he was sleeping. Sophia knew she couldn't last the rest of Winthrop's life hiding her skin from the sun. After another five years at most, they would have to kill off their bunker personas. A contingency plan was already in the works. When the time came, several months before their false deaths, contact with a third bunker would be introduced. Its two inhabitants would attempt to establish an emotional bond with Winthrop by the time Sophia and Derek no longer existed within the narrative. They were both grateful Anjali had the foresight to suggest a disposal chamber for dead bodies during the design stages of the bunker system should they ever need to stagger the deaths of a bunker's inhabitants.

Sophia put on her black jumpsuit, which was made of a thin synthetic fiber. Downward facing vents were built in to make them more breathable in the hot weather. She pulled a black hood over her head, which covered everything but her eyes. Thin gloves, sunglasses, and a black sun hat were the final touches. When she saw her reflection in this outfit, Sophia felt like a beekeeper attending a funeral. She left the building, walking by the parking lot and the executive complex, then took the road winding through the animal enclosures.

Sophia strolled along the field of Armstrongs. Large packs of the cloned black dogs, ranging from puppies to two-year-olds, ran up to her and yelped or barked through the fence for attention. She smiled at them behind the hood and turned back to the road, moving towards the herbivore enclosures.

She followed the route she'd taken with Alistair Holt during her first visit to Phyla. When she was well past the carnivore enclosures and nearing the aviary, she saw Holt driving alone in a jeep to the gate of the Old Dartmouth wall. He used a remote control to open the gate and drove through. It closed behind him.

Sophia had never been one to break the rules, but without giving it a thought, she made her way to the perimeter wall. She needed to find out what was inside. She'd never seen anyone except Holt enter the Old Dartmouth enclosure, so it couldn't be a secret research project because there'd be more people entering and leaving. He never worked alone on projects. He was too busy overseeing all of Phyla's diverse projects and initiatives. Most of his workload was allocated to employees. Plus, Holt had always been so proud and boastful of the work and loved sharing in the process and developing ideas with others. She couldn't imagine what he'd want to hide from them. He let the institute observe and record his own son having sex with a doll, but Old Dartmouth was off limits. She wanted to know what could be so private.

One hundred yards or so to the left of the gate was a tree next to the wall with branches low enough to jump up and get a hold of. She walked over, looking around to make sure nobody was watching, and climbed the tree. After stepping over to the top of the wall, she hung her body over the other side and dropped to the ground. She was at the edge of a forest too thick to see how deep it went. Two black squirrels ran up a red oak tree, one with an acorn, and the other chased behind. Soon six more black squirrels followed them up the tree. Then three more after the six. Then five more after the three. A barred owl was eating a mouse on the branch of a white pine, hidden mostly behind its long dense needles and unfazed by the frantic squirrels or Sophia's presence.

She entered the forest and moved in the general direction of the gate. A red fox crossed in front of her, stopping to observe as if considering her intentions. But a rabbit appeared a few yards away and the fox ran after it. Deeper into the woods, she came upon two deer feeding off the forest floor. A northern flicker drummed its beak on a white pine and the deer ran away. There was so much wildlife packed into such a small area. She saw raccoons, chipmunks, a woodchuck, turkeys, ring-necked pheasant, and a grey fox.

A half-mile into the forest, Sophia approached a clearing, a vast field covering eight to ten acres of land. It seemed out of place, as if she'd just stumbled upon an oasis in the middle of the desert. A small herd of bison grazed the field. Every other species of flora and fauna in the Old Dartmouth enclosure were, at some point, more common to the region. She'd been walking through woods of the South Coast of Massachusetts as it had been in the past until she reached the bison, which was where the experiment showed itself to be a simulation, a living but inauthentic diorama. Holt couldn't help himself. In his fantasy of what the world had been, his favorite animals roamed coastal New England in giant herds as they had the Great Plains. It was history rewritten in a laboratory. Still, she couldn't deny the bison were magnificent. She imagined coming back in winter and watching their breath shoot out their nostrils like they were big organic steam engines, top-heavy and barreling over the frost-crusted earth.

Sophia was mesmerized, momentarily forgetting her mission as if she'd found what she was looking for. She was overwhelmed when one of the larger males trotted towards her, accelerating its pace to declare its dominance on the field. She backed up into the forest and the bison stopped when he reached the tree line but continued to stare at her. With only a few yards between them, the animal looked like a small mountain with legs. Sophia slowly walked deeper into the woods, away from the clearing and around the perimeter of the field. She moved in what she believed was the direction of the road Holt drove in on.

Fifteen minutes and dozens of wildlife encounters later, Sophia reached the road with no sense of how direct her route had been. She observed what appeared to be fresh tire tracks and then turned left. As she proceeded, she kept a few yards of forest between her and the road to stay hidden if Holt drove by. She wondered why more employees hadn't explored the enclosure out of curiosity—it hadn't been so difficult to find a way in and, surely, there were many employees as athletic or more athletic than her, so climbing the tree and dropping down from the top of the wall couldn't be much of a deterrent. But she knew the reason was most Phyla employees were happy with their jobs. The compensation was incredibly generous, and the work was interesting and challenging, so there was no burning collective desire to disobey the few rules Holt imposed. He was a good boss to most.

She began to panic and spiral. What if this was all a huge mistake? What if Bunker 15C was the best thing for Winthrop? What if it was helping him? What if she just needed to see the project through to the end to understand its success? Holt hadn't designed the project, she had. He was a good boss to her. She had autonomous control over any other projects she established at the institute. There weren't any others yet. Bunker 15C was complicated and demanding. Getting the project up and running involved too many different elements and systems working together. They couldn't afford any distractions in the beginning. The little details alone were a constant challenge. It was her responsibility to finish what she'd started. What did she think she was doing trespassing on his private property? She was breaking the law. She was a criminal. She should just turn back and return to the Institute, finish her work for the day and go home to Kelly. No harm done. If she got caught, she'd just tell the truth. Curiosity had gotten the better of her, but once she was inside the enclosure, she realized the mistake she'd made and left immediately. Maybe she would come clean and confess her trespasses to him before she was found out some other way, telling Holt she's been overly anxious about the baby and the success of Bunker 15C. She was having a moment and not establishing any new patterns of behavior. It was an isolated incident. Or perhaps she'd say it was an isolated *occurrence*—incident felt too severe a word to use in the context of trying to downplay what she'd done.

But then she thought about Winthrop going about his day, talking to Penelope and talking to himself, preparing for the next video chat so he'd be interesting enough that they'd want to talk to him again, praying out loud they won't decide not to like him anymore and shut him out.

Sophia subdued her panic attack and resumed her march towards Holt. The land within the Old Dartmouth enclosure was much larger than she anticipated. She'd imagined fifteen to twenty acres at most, but as far as she'd walked already, there'd have been signs of another perimeter wall.

She found his jeep parked off the road in a small clearing between trees. There was no sign of Holt, but the road continued as a footpath, which curved so much she couldn't see where it went. She noticed the faint smell of wood smoke in the air. About a quarter mile down the footpath, there was another clearing. It wasn't as flat and empty as the field with the bison, a handful of trees were scattered around and there was a house. It was the saltbox colonial house Holt had talked about, the one he recreated from the journal written in the 1670s.

It was smaller and more modest than Sophia had pictured in her head. She'd imagined a marriage of colonial authenticity with all the creature comforts and luxuries Holt usually surrounded himself with. But it was a small and basic saltbox, probably not more than one bedroom upstairs, a large room downstairs and a shed in back just under the long side of the roof. The house was painted matte brown not unlike the kinds of pigments used on the houses built in the 17th century. It looked like something from a book about colonial New England. There were three or four windows spaced far apart on each of the exterior walls. They were small windows, indicating a design more concerned with trapping heat than letting in sunlight. A chimney ascended from the center of the roof. The front door was simple, narrow without any decorative frame or overhang, and flush with the exterior wall of the house.

Sophia kept some distance and sat still, observing the house from the woods, taking cover behind several trees and bushes. Initially, there was no sign of Holt, but then he emerged from the house carrying a bucket full of corn and a wooden rocking chair, which he set down on a worn-down patch of ground near the door where a front porch would be. He brought out an identical rocking chair and put it next to the other. He went back inside and returned with an adult-sized doll, seating it in one of the chairs. Holt sat down and began husking the cobs of corn while using his foot to rock the other chair.

Sophia recognized the doll was the same make as Winthrop's Penelope Lorenza companion doll, but this doll was an exact reproduction of Holt's late wife Evelyn who'd died fifteen years earlier of pancreatic cancer. Sophia had seen her photo in Holt's office. He often talked about her and at length. Their life together. Her illness. Holt and the doll were both dressed in clothing styles worn by colonists in early America. Outfits worn by people who worked their own land.

He laughed and joked with the doll. His physical contact was gentle and warm. A hand on her thigh to accompany laughter or placed on top of her hand to share an affectionate moment. He was tender with her. Sophia had never seen this side of him. He was often enthusiastic and positive towards others, but never soft and adoring. The irregularity of his behavior was somewhat disorienting to her. He'd created an alternate world to share with Evelyn. A world neither of them had experienced, a phantom life where her illness and deterioration never happened.

Sophia knew Holt had hired her because she was the most qualified person to run the Bunker 15C Project, but she now felt her presence served two purposes. One for each of Holt's lives. At Phyla, she was one his most valued employees. He'd placed his own son's emotional, mental, and physical health in her hands, trusting her expertise as the best path forward for Winthrop. This was real. But she played a different role in Old Dartmouth. He would never get her to dress in a period Wampanoag outfit, and he knew she would never engage with the reenactment. He wouldn't dare to ask. Nevertheless, his colonial world had a Wampanoag close by and she wondered how often he thought about it. Whenever he spent a few hours during a weekday with Evelyn, whittling or husking while they rocked in the sun, Sophia was likely within a half-mile of their saltbox fantasy.

She contemplated whether deep down he'd wanted her to sneak into the Old Dartmouth enclosure, wandering into the forest and passing through his property as her ancestors had hundreds of years earlier. Sophia halted her stream of consciousness. Attempting to project herself into the thoughts of the man who created this new Old Dartmouth and had potentially projected her as an unknowing participant into his replication was making her sick to her stomach. She sat on the ground, watching Holt and Evelyn and the saltbox. She was upset and needed some time to gather herself before attempting to return to the institute unnoticed. She'd wait until after he left.

It began to drizzle and, soon after, Holt carried Evelyn and the rocking chairs inside. Sophia never once looked at her watch but knew some time had passed. Holt came outside a few times to gather firewood and a bucket of water from the well. When the drizzle turned to heavy rain, he closed the door. Sophia could see the glow from a fire through the first-floor windows and realized Holt wasn't going anywhere. He was staying the night. The residential suite in the executive complex was likely just a place for Holt to shower and change clothes, letting his employees believe it was where he slept the nights he stayed over at Phyla when in fact he spent those nights in the saltbox with Evelyn.

Sophia hadn't brought an umbrella and though her outfit protected her skin from the sunlight, it was not water resistant, and she was getting drenched. She slowly backed up a little deeper into the forest but slipped in a mud puddle and fell to the ground, flat on her stomach. As she pushed herself up out of the mud she saw a shoe, a moccasin, and nearly screamed as she fell backwards into a sitting position. She looked up and two male dolls were posed in front of her, one standing and the other in a crouching position. They both wore deerskin breechcloths and leggings, made to look like Wampanoag men hunting in the late 17th Century. The crouching doll held a bow and arrow while the standing doll wielded a tomahawk. It was too much to absorb all at once. Watching Holt roleplay the past and then seeing her fabricated ancestors posed as if they were souls of the dead trapped for eternity in these fenced-in woods. She stood and walked towards the road, tripping again but catching herself on a tree to keep balance. Every fourth step or so her foot got stuck in the mud. The rain was in a downpour with little protection from the canopy above. Another twenty yards forward, she came upon another doll, a Wampanoag woman in a deerskin skirt and mantle. A few feet further, two young Wampanoag child dolls were poking their heads out from behind a tree as if they were trying not to be seen by passersby. When she was far enough away and out of view from the saltbox, Sophia moved closer to the road hoping it would help her avoid seeing anymore dolls in the forest. She took out her phone in case she needed to use it as a flashlight. She'd silenced it while observing Holt and missed several texts from Derek asking where she was. He'd seen her car was still in the parking lot, but it'd been hours. She responded with the excuse she took a long walk to clear her head and lost track of time, but she was okay, and he shouldn't wait for her. She'd check in with Andrei before she drove home.

The journey back to the perimeter wall took some time even though she followed the road the whole way. Between the rain and mud, not to mention it quickly getting dark out, she needed to walk slowly. Once she reached the perimeter, finding a good spot to cross over was more complicated. With the weather, it'd be easy to slip and fall out of a tree, so she had to find one with ladder-like branches to avoid missing her steps in the dark with nothing but a mobile phone for light. Twenty minutes later, she found a tree with branches close together next to the wall inside the enclosure and slowly made her way back over.

When she returned to the institute, Andrei was sitting at the long table, sipping iced coffee and running a diagnostic report of Bunker 15C's systems for HVAC, oxygen levels, humidity, carbon monoxide and radiation detection.

"Yo, Sophia," he said. "Why are you here so late?"

"I lost track of time," she said, looking at the monitors. She was dripping water all over the floors. Winthrop was sitting on the couch viewing the wall screen with Penelope. "What's he doing?"

"Watching the virtual night sky with Penelope," Andrei said without looking up from his own work. "He's identifying constellations for her. He knows a lot of them. He named twenty-six so far. It's kind of impressive."

Sophia walked over to a desk and picked up an empty envelope and sealed it shut.

"Andrei, could you take this over to the executive complex and put it in the drop box outside Holt's office?"

"I'm kind of in the middle of something," Andrei said, looking up at her for the first time. "You're really wet."

"Andrei, it's important he sees it first thing in the morning and I have some things to finish up before I go home," she said. "Free snacks on me for two months."

"Ok. Fine," he said, not as aggravated as he wanted to sound. He took the envelope from her. "But don't touch this laptop. I don't want to have to run this report again."

"Thank you," she said.

When he'd gone, she changed out of her protective suit, then put her laptop and a few files in her bag and looked around. She watched Winthrop smile and point to a constellation, telling Penelope it was called Andromeda. Sophia walked over to one of the shared terminals and typed a series of commands, then clicked the mouse three times. Several loud sustained beeps sounded off throughout the Bunker 15C research center. On the monitors, Winthrop looked in the opposite direction of the wall screens.

Sophia left the building and drove home.

The large door to Bunker 15C opened. Winthrop poked his head out, peering suspiciously into the cavernous and brightly-lit space housing the bunker. Workstations on wheels were scattered around carrying half-empty coffee mugs and monitors displaying data readings. A hospital gurney and emergency medical station was set up in one corner. White lab coats hung from hooks along the wall next to a door with a red-lettered exit sign mounted above.

Winthrop walked further out into the space.

"Hello?"

There was no response.

"Hello?" he repeated.

PART II

SPARE PARTS

HOLYOKE

In former Western Massachusetts, a village composed of dozens of large campfires had been established on the bank of a half-mile stretch of the Connecticut River. Somebody had nailed a found sign with the word "Holyoke" to a tree, so that's what people called the village. There was never any ceremony to make it official, but Holyoke took. For the most part, spots around the fires were first come, first served each night. There were some fires with permanent residents. They tended to be nicer with better stones and seating and more space for each individual spot. These claims were rarely challenged because their inhabitants either served a greater community purpose or offered a popular service, and they were protected. Most of the population was made up of travelers, nomads, and those who were never sure whether they were staying or going even though they'd likely been in Holyoke for some time. It had become a neutral zone, a good place to stop for a day or two for those making their way to the Atlantic coast, or those running away from it. The fires, which were always going, provided warmth year-round. Rain and snow complicated things and when the weather was bad people would leave for a day or two in hopes of finding shelter, but many had tents and would stay. The permanent residents started constructing large, vented boxes made of corrugated tin to place over the fires when the rain or snow was heavy to keep them from going out—the heat conducted by all the boxes also provided some warmth for those who didn't leave.

The permanent residents were clustered together in a circle of campfires called the Nucleus. There was enough room around these fires to allow space for sleeping tents. The perimeter fires of the Nucleus were home to the strongest men and women in Holyoke. They chopped the firewood and served as a security force for the village. Some of the residents inside the circle were builders and craftspeople, constructing the tin boxes, building tents and furniture, welding, and making or mending clothes when needed. Others went out gathering supplies from nearby urban ruins. Hunters and gardeners inhabited several fires, and two fires were reserved for doctors and nurses.

The largest fire pit was the most popular in Holyoke. It was made up of a half dozen smaller campfires, which were inhabited and operated by the Spice Family. They were nine: siblings Brother Spice and Sister Spice, Brother's wife, and each sibling had three children. Holyoke had been founded by the Spice Family ten years after people started leaving the bunkers. Brother and Sister Spice had spent all their time and resources before settling Holyoke acquiring spices, seasonings, cookware, kitchen utensils, and culinary knowledge, be it from old cookbooks or food magazines or word of mouth recipes. They accumulated as much as they could and bartered generously for every item and piece of information. Many thought they were crazy, putting everything into gathering flavors and mastering different cooking techniques instead focusing on the skills and materials necessary for long-term survival, wondering who needs a chinois or mandolin slicer when medical equipment and engine fuel were so hard to come by. But they built a village around their cooking. Even in the worst of times everybody enjoys a good meal. The Spice Family Fire Pit was one of the only operating restaurants in Old New England and everybody who sampled their cooking thought it was beyond compare.

They worked on a barter system. A customer could bring them game, fish, and vegetables to cook and the Spice Family would provide the flavoring and basic food staples like vinegar and cooking fats; in exchange, half of the prepared food would be given to members of the Nucleus. If the customer had no food, then they would have to offer something else to barter for a meal, which could be something material or worked off through labor. If the customer had a skill set necessary for the community's survival, they might be invited to join the Nucleus.

The biggest project underway was the construction of a defensive wall around the community, a timber palisade. As Holyoke became more popular, the influx of visitors grew, which meant more noise and stronger odors carried off in the wind. It attracted predators and there had been some attacks. They'd killed a couple tigers and a grizzly bear over the past year, but at least a dozen people died from animal attacks. Some of their hunters had seen a large jaguar stalking around the nearby woods. The palisade would protect them against large predatory animals. It would also offer some relief for the nighttime security watch. The number of guards on duty overnight could be reduced by spreading them out on observation platforms along the top of the palisade and equipping them with bells to use as an alarm system.

Additionally, the palisade would allow members of the Nucleus to control the population of Holyoke on any given night to avoid the skirmishes and arguments inevitable when there weren't enough spots around the fires for everyone who showed up. Nights with a large influx of guests overextended the security force, which created a domino effect leading to overall vulnerability and less firewood. With the wall in place, they would be able to close and lock the gates for the night once the chosen capacity had been reached. Holyoke would be safer and more peaceful for Nucleus members and visitors alike. Sister Spice was often heard saying, "The palisade is an architecture for the greater good."

HELICOPTERS

The girl was alone. She was seventeen years old if she was keeping track of time accurately and had been moving from place to place, hunting and scavenging, since her mother died of an unknown illness outside of Albany two months prior, but from what she'd gleaned from books and old magazines, she suspected it was some kind of cancer. The last time she saw her father was about a month before her mother passed away. He'd gone off searching for doctors, hoping to find someone to identify and treat his wife's illness, but he never returned. She knew something must have happened to him. Her father wasn't the abandoning type. She vowed to her mother's corpse that she would find him.

The girl had heard about Holyoke from two brothers who'd been overnight guests at the campfires a few times. Their names were Grady and Bo. They told her she looked nice, then tried to rob her and maybe worse, but she took a finger from each of them with her hatchet and claw hammer. She told them she had no desire to take anything else and they went on their way. Holyoke sounded like the kind of place her father had been looking for, so she set off for the village hoping to find somebody there who'd met him.

She buried most of her possessions and weapons about a half

mile away from the community and marked it, taking just enough to protect herself—her claw hammer, a hunting knife, and two box cutters. As well as some goods for trading or bartering: a half dozen unused fish hooks, a roll of duct tape, and five large rabbits she'd trapped and killed that morning.

When she arrived at the campfires, there was no security check-in, which meant no one looked through her things or frisked her, so she could keep her weapons. But she noticed at least four large men and women, armed with baseball bats and shotguns, watching her closely as she walked over to claim a spot at a campfire not far from the Nucleus. There were signs attached to sawhorses scattered around the village warning that anyone who's caught stealing someone else's possessions or campfire spot for the evening will be escorted out of the village and banished for six months.

While she settled in, she met a couple of the others sharing her campfire for the night. To her right was Harry, who was probably her father's age or older. He was no more than five foot two and stout with long dark brown hair braided in pigtails with a full beard ending somewhere below his collarbone. He had forearms thick as thighs and told her most people called him Hare Bear. He talked a lot. To her left was Biv, who appeared roughly her age. They were tall and slim, wearing a long gray canvas coat and a black wool skullcap over their shaved head. They didn't talk as much as Hare Bear, but they weren't unfriendly.

"This place is great," said Hare Bear as he rubbed his palms together more to keep his hands busy than to warm them. "I stay here most of the time. Doubt I'll ever be invited to join the Nucleus. Probably too much of a loudmouth for them, but I'm a pretty good hunter and don't cause any trouble. So long as I never stay too long in one campfire spot or linger where I'm not supposed to linger, they don't mind. This is my favorite season. Not too warm, so I'll sleep well. The leaves will start changing colors soon. Doesn't smell as bad as it does in the summer around here. What'd you say your name was again?"

A strong gust of wind swept through the village and the girl noticed dozens of samaras falling from the trees above. Hare Bear tore a few in half and threw them up in the air to watch them helicopter down into the fire.

"Maple," the girl said. "My name is Maple."

"I like that," Hare Bear said. "Maple is a good name. I like names that are already names of things. Makes them familiar, like I've known you in a different form before. And I like trees. I like them more than bushes or flowers."

Biv nodded in agreement with Hare Bear's sentiment.

"What's that around your neck?" the girl asked Biv, pointing to the bronze pendant they were wearing.

"Family heirloom," Biv answered, moving the pendant inside their shirt to conceal it. "It's not of any real value."

"Don't worry," the girl said. "I was just making conversation. It looks good on you."

"Maple," Hare Bear uttered to get her attention. "What brings you this way? Is Holyoke your destination or just a short stop on your journey?"

"I don't know," she said. "I'm looking for my father."

The girl took out a drawing her mother did of her father and handed it to Hare Bare. Her mother had been a good artist, with a special talent for portraits. The drawing looked just like her father.

"My mother was very ill, and my father left our camp in search of doctors who might be able to help her," the girl said. "When my mother died, I set out to find him. Have you seen him around here recently?"

"I'm awfully sorry about your mother," Hare Bear said and then concentrated on the drawing. "Yeah, I remember him. We didn't share a campfire, so I never talked to him, but he was here for maybe two days. It was at least six to eight weeks ago. I'm sure I saw him talking to the doctors who live in the Nucleus. They might know more about where he was heading after Holyoke. Seemed like a nice fella from a distance."

"Thank you," she said. "Do you two have food for dinner tonight?"

"Not yet," Hare Bear said. "But we always find something."

Biv nodded in agreement.

"You can share my rabbit with me," the girl said. "Keep an eye on my things while I'm gone."

The girl picked up the rabbits and left the campfire. She walked around for a while to scope out the village before she approached the Nucleus. Everyone seemed to behave themselves. The only violence she witnessed was a soft and sloppy fistfight between two drunks. Even though there was no official rule of law, the security force was the closest thing to an organized militia the girl had seen in quite some time. They had a vibe about them like anyone who caused a disruption was going to be escorted out to the middle of the woods and forced to dig their own grave. She knew it would be in her best interest not to cop an attitude towards them, which was challenging for her. It wasn't in her nature to be polite. She'd had little experience with etiquette and other people aside from her parents.

When the girl walked up to the Spice Family Fire Pit, Sister Spice's teenage daughter Harriet was handling transactions. The girl presented the rabbits, asking for one to be cooked for her for dinner and the others smoked and made into jerky to take with her on the road, offering two whole rabbits as payment. She asked to talk to the doctors who lived in the Nucleus and said she'd give them the fifth rabbit as a gift for their time. Harriet walked over to her mother to relay the message. Sister Spice approached the girl, picked up the rabbits, sizing her up before she said anything.

"Are you sick?" Sister Spice asked.

"No," the girl answered.

"Then why do you want to talk to our doctors?"

"I'm looking for my father," the girl answered. "My mother was ill, and he went looking for doctors to help her. I have reason to believe he came through Holyoke. If he did, he would've tried to talk to the doctors."

"Where's your mother now?" Sister Spice asked.

"She died."

"I'm sorry to hear that," Sister Spice said. "And you just want to talk to the doctors."

"I only want a few minutes of their time to figure out if they met my father and if they know where he went."

"What's your name?" Sister Spice asked.

"Maple," the girl said.

"You look more like a pit bull to me, but Maple's nice. It's a pretty name," Sister Spice said. She wore a playful smile as she said it. "Go over and sit in that chair next to the rotisserie and turn the spit for me, slowly. I'll make sure our doctors come over and talk to you. You can still have half the fifth rabbit. You want it cooked for tonight or smoked to last?

"Smoked," the girl answered.

"The jerky won't be ready until the day after tomorrow," Sister Spice said. "This is a good yield for a day's work. All five are fresh kills and some big meaty rabbits too. If you're ever looking for a more permanent arrangement, room can always be made in the

Nucleus for a good hunter."

"Thanks," the girl said. "I'll think about it."

"I know, I know," Sister Spice responded. "You need to go off and find your Dad. Think of it as a standing offer."

Sister Spice walked away, taking the rabbits with her. The girl sat down in the chair and turned the rotisserie as she waited for the doctors. It was a long spit skewering three young hogs over the fire. It smelled like smoky heaven.

A while later, Sister Spice returned with a tall and thin man wearing a beige trench coat with a stethoscope hanging around his neck. He looked like the living dead.

"I'm Doc Flanders," he said. He was curt but not unfriendly. His face was long and sunken, his skin was pale and his eyes had a sleepy gaze. "You wanted to ask me about someone?"

"My father," the girl answered, handing her mother's drawing to him. "He went off in search of doctors to help my mother."

Doc Flanders studied the drawing closely.

"It's a wonderful drawing," he said.

"My mother drew it a while before he left," the girl said.

"I remember him," Doc Flanders said. "He passed through Holyoke maybe two months ago, give or take. Was looking for a doctor who could help your mother. He described the symptoms of her illness, which sounded like cancer to me, and I told him it would be hard to know how to treat her without some sort of imaging tech. We might have a serviceable general medicine practice for Holyoke, but we don't have the kind of facility needed to treat terminal illnesses."

"Do have any idea where he went from here?" The girl asked.

"I told your father some of the bunkers that are still operational might have advanced medical facilities," he responded. "He said he had heard someone talking about large bunker communities east of here near the ocean, but I advised him against engaging those groups. The rumors about those communities are disturbing."

"What kind of rumors?" the girl asked.

"Body transplants, forced surgeries, mutilations," he said. "Nothing good and certainly not the kind of help he was seeking. But he was desperate, and I think he probably headed east."

"Do you know exactly where they're located?" she asked.

"I do not," he said. "And I wouldn't tell you if I did. You don't want to go there. No good will come of it."

"I'm going to find him," the girl says. "He's all I have left now."

"Well," Doc Flanders said. "I wish you all the luck in the world."

He shuffled off briskly, disappearing into a group of people waiting to see him.

"He's right you know," Sister Spice added. "You do not want to go where you're designing to go."

"I have to," the girl said.

"It's a fool's expedition," Sister Spice said. "But you're gonna go anyway and I kind of like you. Kind of. So, I'll lend you some supplies and necessities, but you'll need to return whatever's leftover if you live."

"Thanks."

"You're a stubborn little thing, aren't you?" Sister Spice said. "Want to try some of that rotisserie hog? Should be just right."

The girl ate the few pieces Sister Spice sliced off and handed to her. It was the most delicious mouthful she'd ever tasted. Flavors and spices she'd never known before. Sister Spice told her to come back for her dinner in four hours. They were making a rabbit and blood stew with rosemary, potatoes, and onion. She tossed a small canvas sack to the girl.

"That's some of our secret salt. On the house," she said. "It makes everything taste better."

CIVET DE LAPIN

Hare Bear's beard had trapped so much stew it glistened with the campfire's reflection. He sucked every drop out while he waited for the girl to offer seconds. Biv laughed at him as they took their time with their portion.

"Oh, this is good," Hare Bear said, folding his beard up to his mouth to lick. "Really good. Many thanks to you for sharing. This is the best dish I've ever had from the Spice Family and I've had so many. She must really like you. There's more meat than one rabbit here, so I don't think Nucleus took its full share. There were five rabbits and three are being smoked. I guess they could give you less than one and a half of the smoked rabbits, but that's not their style. It's always half of everything offered."

"Hare Bear," the girl interrupted. "Would you like another helping?"

"Yes, please," he responded. "But only if it'll go to waste. I don't mean to take more than you want to give."

"There's plenty," the girl said, scooping some more into his bowl.

"How long are you staying for?" Biv asked.

"The jerky will be ready the day after tomorrow and then I'll head due east to the coast," the girl answered. "I think my father went that way hoping to find some groups with more advanced medical equipment."

"Did the Spices warn you about the coast?" Hare Bear asked.

"They did."

"It's bad news to the east," he said. "Ruled by the Winthrops and the Phoenixes. You don't want to mess around with either of them."

"Have you been to their camps?" the girl asked.

"No," he said. "But I've crossed paths with both. Lucky for me they were in a big messy rumble with each other when I did."

"What do you know about them?" the girl asked.

"Well…"

SCYLLA & CHARYBDIS

"...from what I've been told, they were both established before they entered the bunkers, so they're old. Other than that, I know nothing of their time in the bunker or before. Not sure I want to. Maybe a year ago or more I was making my way to the ocean. I'd been here for a spell and it was nice, but I'd heard there were more communities on the coast and thought I'd scout 'em out to see if there might be some spot offering a more permanent situation for me. A place to settle down. The journey from here to there was treacherous. Predators around every corner. Lucky for me I climb trees real fast like a squirrel or monkey. If I wasn't built abnormal like I am, I would've been dinner a dozen times or so. It also helps I have a quick hand with my machete and mini sledge. Still, I was terrified. There was a tiger at one point had me trapped way up in a hemlock tree, further than he was willing to go, especially after I cracked him good between the eyes with the mini sledge. He must have fallen twenty feet and then waited on the ground for me, circling around the base of the trunk. Fortunately, a troupe of boar came charging through and that tiger went after them. It took some doing, but I eventually made it to the coast in one piece. Heard a commotion one day and came upon a battle like I'd never seen before. It was brutal and relentless. It was a proper battle like in stories and books about wars and castles. There were thirty or forty people going at each other. No one noticed little ole me, so I scurried up a tree and watched from a distance, I didn't even notice what kind of tree it was. Deciduous, I think. Anyway, the one side who were fewer, which I now know was the Winthrop Clan, looked normal enough like they could be walking amongst us here at Holyoke on the security force or chopping wood. They might have been fewer in number, but they had more firepower. Word has it they make their own ammo and not just scattershot for shotguns, but real bullets. And I've seen their hardware firsthand: hunting rifles, bolt action, semi-automatic assault rifles and pistols, revolvers, and more than I have names for. Supposedly, though I can't vouch for the reliability of this information, they have explosives experts who can make rockets and grenades and all that, not just the pipe bombs and leg shredders we usually come across. Real high-tech warfare coming from the Winthrop Clan. They were mean and skilled on the battlefield. They don't just have the good weapons; they know how to use them right. I know you're wondering to yourself, "How was this much of a battle, Hare Bear? How did it last more than thirty seconds? Bullets are bullets and that should be the end of it." I tell you what, I wouldn't mess with the Winthrop Clan any day of the week. They are fierce and terrifying and would just as soon riddle me with one hundred bullets as look at me. But the Phoenix House, they are a different thing altogether. A breed of people born out of nightmares. All the stories I'd heard at Holyoke were true. I'd rather die a thousand deaths than fall into their hands. They don't want to kill you, at least not at first. They want to take you apart piece by piece, and then rebuild each other with all your parts. Looking at them on that battlefield, each of them was made up of different parts of different people. Two separate ears, neither original. Hands, arms, legs, and feet all from different people. But all on one body. And they all wear the same coveralls, mostly gray. I don't know how they do it, but I do know that if you're a member of the Phoenix House, you're either a hunter or a surgeon. And they're zealots, like all their butchery is bringing them closer to some god. I've heard they all answer to some prophet who's called the Collage. They might not have as much firepower, but there were more of them and none of them was afraid of dying. Charge straight at an assault rifle with nothing but a baseball bat and bike chain. They did have shotguns and some deadly archers, so it wasn't all melee against machine guns. The whole experience was the ugliest thing I ever saw. Just blood and guts all over the place. It stained the ground beneath them. I didn't stick around until it was over, so I never knew the final tally. A Phoenix hunter saw me descending the tree and chased me into the woods. When she got close, she told me she liked my thick arms and wanted to share them with the house. Like many often do because of my size, she underestimated my speed and strength. She half-assed her attack, coming in slow and exposed. She swung her nail-spiked baseball bat at my head but missed and I was able to get one deep hack at her jugular with the machete before she had time to swing again. I was lucky she missed and even luckier she was alone. I ran deeper into the woods until I found a small settlement on the ocean. Four or five structures in all. Houses and buildings. The man in charge said most people called him the Salt-maker, but that his name was Emmett. He and his family harvest and trade sea salt. He was friendly and unafraid. He showed me around, pointing to a stretch of salt evaporation ponds beyond the buildings. I asked if he was with either of the groups I'd seen and he told me no, that his family operated independently, but he knew them. They didn't bother him for the same reason no one bothered him because they loved his salt, and no one, not the Winthrops or Phoenixes or any other roamers who might otherwise murder anyone who had something they wanted, not a one of them wanted to put in the labor involved into harvesting and processing sea salt. They could probably figure out how to do it, but it wouldn't leave enough time for marauding and feuding or feasting and drinking and screwing. So, they left him alone so long as he gave them salt. He knew well enough who to make happy and who he could demand and barter with. He provided them with all the salt they could ever want in exchange for protection and refraining from terrorizing any member of his family. He said he was like one of those birds he'd seen in his nature books who perched in crocodiles' mouths and cleaned the crocs' teeth by feeding off the stuck bits of flesh and river muck, and so because of this service they offered, the crocs didn't eat them. He and his children would travel to a handful of communities and settlements further inland to trade salt for all the other goods and treats they need to live a comfortable salt-making existence. In fact, they were in the middle of harvesting some large batches when I encountered him. A few of his children had fallen ill and they had a large delivery due, which needed three people to handle. One to steer the carriage and the other two to keep eyes out for thieves and large predators, more to protect the horse than anyone else. They only had the one horse. Emmett had to stay back to tend to his sick children, so he offered me safe passage to Holyoke if I helped his son and daughter transport the salt to the Spice Family. They could move faster without the salt, so they wouldn't need me on the way back. Well, I'd had my fill of the coast and felt I may have made myself a target, not knowing if any of the other Phoenixes had seen me, so I enthusiastically accepted the offer. His daughter Emma warned me if I tried anything funny she'd use her shotgun to paint the woods with my face, which didn't scare me too much after what I'd just seen. She wasn't going to wear my arms like they were her arms or anything, so I kept my eyes open and mouth shut all the way back to Holyoke. Spotted a couple wolves and a leopard for them. Did my job and kissed the ground when we got here. Haven't strayed very far since. The ocean shores are all full of evil, Maple."

BEST FRIENDS FOREVER

"So, you said the Phoenix House has surgeons?" the girl asked.

"Well, yeah," Hare Bear said. "They're amputating body parts head to toe and reattaching them to each other. Every one of them I saw with my own eyes had several of these surgeries, and I think I only saw a small platoon of them. They must have a big team of doctors performing all these operations, maybe a couple dozen. Maybe more. I don't really know how many Phoenixes there are total."

Hare Bear looked down into his bowl of stew and ate a spoonful. He was avoiding eye contact with the girl.

"Did you hear anything about their medical facilities?" the girl asked.

"No," he answered. "I don't think they share the inner workings of their slaughterhouse with the public, but I imagine they have better facilities than most. I bet they're fancy and state-of-the-art, or whatever that meant in the bunkers and before. It's been their way since then. It's what they do best. You should stay away from them."

"That's where my father went," the girl said. "So I have to go there."

"Maple," Biv interjected. "You really shouldn't."

"Should or shouldn't is irrelevant to me," she said.

"Then, you shouldn't go alone," they said.

"Are you offering your services?" the girl said. "You barely know me, and you certainly shouldn't trust me."

"I'm not afraid," they said. "And I need a change of scenery. Don't we, Hare Bear?"

"This is a bad idea," Hare Bear said.

"I'm not asking anyone to join me," the girl said.

Hare Bear stared into his stew as he were searching for an escape route. "Fine. I think I know my way back to the Salt-maker and that's the safest place on the coast," he said. "I prefer to stay close to Biv, seeing as we're accustomed to looking out for each other. Plus, you gave me two portions of stew. It'd be rude not to help, but I don't need a change of scenery. This is good scenery. It's warm and safe."

The girl served Hare Bear a third helping of stew. She thanked them both and then laid down on her mother's favorite wool blanket, clutching a box cutter in each hand.

WE'LL MEET AGAIN

Sister Spice walked out of the Nucleus with three security force members following just behind her. She moved slowly, which gave everybody in her path plenty of time to get out of the way and give her some space. She never asked them to move out of the way nor did she expect them to, but they always did. The girl, Hare Bear, and Biv were packing up to leave when she found them.

"Maple," Sister Spice beckoned. "Here's your smoked rabbit jerky. One's got black pepper for flavor and the other's sugar and jalapeno powder."

She handed the girl two sacks and sized up her crew.

"You didn't have to deliver it," the girl said. "I'd have gotten it."

"I know I didn't," Sister Spice said. "But I needed to get my legs moving and wanted to wish you well on your travels, which I still believe to be ill-advised."

"Me too," Hare Bear jumped in. "Why leave? There's food and warmth and to the east nothing but trouble. I was just telling her about the trip I made to the ocean to see what was there. It was maybe a year ago or more."

Sister Spice gave Hare Bear the coldest look she had to offer, raising one eyebrow high to communicate her displeasure. He stopped talking and took a few steps back.

"As I was saying," Sister Spice said. "Ill-advised. But it's your life."

"Is that salt you gave me from the Salt-maker on the coast?" the girl asked.

"It is," Sister Spice answered.

"We're going that way," the girl said. "Is there anything you want me to deliver to him?"

"No," Sister Spice said. The edges of her mouth curled into a devilish smile. "Emmett can come get what I have to give him when he brings me some of his special salt. Tell him I said hello."

She handed the girl a larger backpack filled with goods. The girl was confused by the gift and said as much with her eyes.

"Some more provisions for you," Sister Spice clarified. "You and your friends, even Mr. Bear the talk-box over there, always have a place here at Holyoke. Might even have some openings in the Nucleus when you return. There'd be room for your father too."

"Why?" the girl asked.

"Safe travels," Sister Spice said as she walked back towards the Nucleus. The small crowd of people waiting for campfire vacancies parted like the Red Sea to let Sister Spice and her security crew pass through.

"She must love you like kin to offer us all spots in the Nucleus," Hare Bear said. "Because I'm sure she doesn't like me very much."

"You're just an acquired taste," the girl said. "I hid a duffel bag of my things in the woods. Let's grab it and make our way east."

HAPPY TRAILS

The walk from Holyoke to the Atlantic lasted a week and a half. They didn't rush knowing they'd need their strength for what lay ahead, so there was no skimping on sleep or breaks to rest their legs.

They got to know each other better observing each other's daily habits without the distractions and chaos of Holyoke. Less energy had to be expended on looking over one's shoulder to make sure no one was trying to steal your possessions. It was the closest thing to friendship the girl had ever experienced outside of her parents, but she remained weary and didn't sleep easily. She noticed Biv often rubbed their temples when no one was looking.

"Do you have bad migraines?" the girl asked.

"No," Biv said. "Just some exercises I do to quiet my mind."

"Quiet it from what?" the girl asked.

"It's just some anxiety," Biv answered.

Hare Bear often cried in his sleep. A couple nights he was sobbing and shaking so bad they had to wake him. He'd jerk up half awake and half in a nightmare screaming out, "I don't. I don't. Please. I don't know how. Leave me alone." The night terrors were the only aspect of his life he didn't want to talk about.

The girl learned Hare Bear and Biv had partnered up roughly

a year earlier, not long after Hare Bear returned from his visit to the east coast. Neither had any other friends or family when they met at one of the campfires. They'd talked about how lonely and exhausting it was being on guard constantly, never having a single night to sleep soundly, living in fear of being alone forever or getting robbed and attacked for less than you were willing to give away freely. They made a pact to look out for each other and always keep company and hadn't spent a night apart since.

During their journey to the Salt-maker, no tigers or jaguars were seen, but they saw a black bear cub and its mother, a wolf, a lynx, and a few coyotes. They had a tense standoff with a lone hyena, but eventually it walked away from the confrontation, and they didn't see it again. Sister Spice had packed them some ground coffee, brown sugar, bread, cheese, salami, carrots, potatoes, and butter in the backpack. They hunted rabbits and squirrels along the way. Biv caught two rainbow trout in a stream north of Worcester on day three with their fly rod. It had been their father's favorite pastime. He'd shown them how to tie their own flies and which flies to use as bait for which fish and how to move and manipulate them once they hit the water.

It was almost like a vacation. No other people to contend with or worry about. Just three friends and the elements making their way to the killing floor by the sea.

The girl wished she knew. She wished she could be a little bird for a day, a sparrow or nuthatch, and fly to search every nook and cranny both the Winthrop Clan and Phoenix House laid claim to and find out whether her father was dead or alive. If he were alive, it'd be an easy decision. Rescue him from whoever had him or die trying. Revenge would be her first impulse if he were dead, but she was thinking maybe getting the three of them involved in what was sure to be a long and drawn-out suicide mission would serve no greater purpose. Maybe it'd be better not to die or be chopped up and then sewn on to the bodies of her own captors. Maybe it'd be better to keep walking and sleeping and fishing and cooking. Maybe it'd be better to worry about soothing Hare Bear out of his night terrors or help Biv quiet their mind. Maybe it'd be better to go back to Holyoke and see what the Nucleus was all about—she liked Sister Spice, but there was something off about the whole arrangement. Why'd Sister Spice like her so much? She was curious about people who gave things to her. She wanted to trust Hare Bear and Biv, but she'd never trusted anyone but her parents. She contemplated these alternate scenarios like counting sheep until she fell asleep.

THE SALT-MAKER

The family was raking salt into little mounds in the evaporation ponds when the girl and her two companions arrived. When the Salt-maker saw Hare Bear, he waved them over enthusiastically. His body language was welcoming and relaxed. His behavior was unsettling to the girl. He seemed to be from a different time and place, though she had no sense of where and when. He carried no fear of the outside world with him. His children were more cautious. They quickly moved closer to their father, picking up whatever could be used as a weapon. The girl heard the pump action of a shotgun behind her.

"Please drop whatever you're holding, put your arms up and do not, I repeat, do not turn around," Emma the Salt-maker's daughter ordered.

"Emma," the Salt-maker called out. "Don't be so aggressive. These are friends. You remember Mr. Hare Bear. You told me he'd been very helpful delivering the salt to Holyoke."

"You can be friendly if you want," Emma responded. "But I don't know the other two."

"Mr. Salt-maker," Hare Bear greeted warmly. "So good to see you again."

"You know that's not my name," the Salt-maker said. "Please call me Emmett."

"Okay Emmett," Hare Bear said with a blush. "These are my friends Maple and Biv. Maple's looking for her father and thinks he might have passed through these parts."

"Have you seen him?" the girl asked, handing the drawing of her father to the Salt-maker.

The Salt-maker looked closely at the image. His face changed.

"Yes," he answered somberly. "He passed through here a while ago. Said he wanted to find somebody with advanced medical training and facilities. I told him the only groups around here with that kind of infrastructure are the Winthrop Clan and the Phoenix House, but to stay away. I told him a quick death was the best-case scenario on the other side of those two groups."

The girl asked if he knew where her father went, hoping the Salt-maker would surprise her and say her father heeded his warning and headed back west in search of an alternative solution. But she knew where her father had gone. She knew while she sat for days next to her mother's corpse that he wouldn't return to them until he found a miracle cure for the death growing inside his wife. She also knew there was no bad decision he wouldn't make to avoid accepting the inevitable truth: there was no cure, there was only dying and being there for the dying. So, the girl had observed the death alone, then days later cremated the body in a bonfire under the night sky. All she had left of her mother was the wool blanket, the drawing of her father, and a pill box filled with some of the ashes. It was antique silver embellished with a wolf's head, her mother's favorite animal. They'd found it while scavenging for pain-killers and matches in downtown Albany.

"He didn't give me the impression he was going to turn back," the Salt-maker said. "And I haven't seen him since."

"Maybe he went southwest to somewhere like Old Connecticut," Hare Bear said in an attempt at optimism. "I've heard New Haven used to be real smart. They could have some good doctors."

"He didn't go to New Haven," the girl said. "Where do these groups live?"

"You don't want to take that path," the Salt-maker said. "You're young and healthy. That's a gift in this world."

The girl insisted. Since there was no dissuading her, the Salt-maker advised she approach the Winthrop Clan first. If she surrendered her weapons and just asked for a brief audience with the Council of Chiefs, they might not kill her.

"Their intentions aren't what I would call conventionally noble," he said, "but under the right circumstances, there is the possibility of conversation."

"What about the Phoenix House?" the girl asked.

"If you discover that they have your father," he responded, "go back to Holyoke. They'll capture you and your friends, then butcher you slowly so they can show you where the parts they've taken from you have gone. The Collage likes an audience."

"Who is the Collage?" the girl asked.

"He's their leader," The Salt-maker said. "They call him a prophet. Never seen his face without the mask and headdress on, but I've met him. You need to be careful around him. Anything that might be construed as disrespectful by his followers, his 'kindred', will get you thrown into one of their animal pits once they remove what they want from you."

"Animal pits?" the girl asked.

"Yes, they have five big pits, each with a different species," he said. "One's got a half dozen raccoons, another has two hyenas, then usually a pack of pit bulls in another. I think they also had a brown bear and a few boars in the other two last time I saw the pits. I imagine these animals eventually die of malnutrition. They starve them to make them more aggressive and desperate. Whenever they want to make an example of someone, they throw them in one of the pits. There's even a wheel they spin to decide which animal you get thrown to."

"How do you know so much about them?" the girl asked.

"Every year they hold a ceremony and celebration of the Phoenix House called The Festival of New Skin," The Salt-maker said. "The Collage always requests my family's presence. One doesn't turn down an invitation from him. I've seen a lot of things I wish I'd never seen, which I could go on about, but the only advice I have is to stay away from them."

"I need to find my father," she said.

"I can't stop you," he said with a sigh. "But let me make a feast for us tonight. My son Rudy caught some striped bass today and I have a recipe for salt-baked fish from Sister Spice that is simply to die for. As fine a meal as any to send you off to meet your maker."

THE RING OF WINTHROP

The girl approached the Clan's fortress alone. Hare Bear and Biv hid in some woods nearby with a view of the structure. It was large, at least a quarter mile in diameter, with a design based on old Viking ring fortresses. The perimeter wall was fifteen feet tall and made of oak posts. Clan members armed with rifles stood guard every fifty feet or so along the inner walkway at the top of the wall. The girl walked towards one of the gated entrances with her arms up. She'd decided against going unarmed, knowing they'd be more suspicious if she had no weapons on her than a few she was willing to surrender. She left her favorite hatchet and claw hammer with Hare Bear so she wouldn't lose them if she had to make a quick escape.

The Winthrop clanswoman standing guard just above the gate put up her hand to halt the girl. She was muscular and had her shoulder-length black hair in a ponytail held down by a camouflage baseball cap. There was a laid-back confidence in her body language, a warrior's swagger.

"Can I help you?" the Winthrop clanswoman asked.

"I'm looking for someone," the girl answered.

"Who?"

"My father," the girl said. "I have it on good authority that he passed through the area, and I've been told your Council of Chiefs would know if he had."

"Oh," the Winthrop clanswoman said. "And who told you that?"

"Not my father," the girl said.

The Winthrop clanswoman shook her head and chuckled.

"You're funny," she said. "But you better watch that shit. Some of my comrades here don't share my sense of humor. I'll go ask if the Council will grant you an audience. While I'm gone, stand where you are or the sentries will fill you with holes. They're not good at much, but putting holes in people is kind of their thing. What's your name?"

"Maple."

"Hi, Maple," the Winthrop clanswoman said. "My name is Rosita. Rosita Winthrop."

The girl waited for forty-five minutes until the gate opened for her. Rosita greeted her with four armed guards. After patting her down and taking the boxcutter and tire iron she had on with her, they escorted her to see the Council. A small busy village existed inside the gates with an almost military order to all its activity, unlike the festive chaos in Holyoke. Half the space was used for agricultural purposes and even the farmers moved and operated in drill-like formations as they tended and harvested the crops. The other half made up the village proper. Several longhouses served as the primary architecture with little shacks offering food and day-to-day necessities scattered throughout.

"Are you related to the founder of the Winthrop Clan?" the girl asked Rosita.

"Not by blood," Rosita answered. "We all take on the last name Winthrop, whether we're born into it or recruited."

The girl observed that the longhouses couldn't account for

enough space to act as both residences and meeting spaces for all the people she saw. There was one cabin that couldn't have been much larger than 12x12 feet inside and was guarded by three heavily armed sentries. The girl believed it to be the entrance to the underground bunker they had originally emerged from. She was guided to a longhouse next to the cabin.

Inside the longhouse were no fewer than twenty armed sentries. A long table on a raised platform seated three men and three women, the Council of Chiefs. There was no other furniture inside and the décor was modest except for a dozen framed movie posters hanging on the walls, placed uniformly as if they were paintings of former council members. Four of the posters were for movies starring an actress named Penelope Lorenza: *Dangerous Connections, When We Were Yesterday, The Warlock's Lover,* and *House of Shadows.* The other posters were from older classic films: *The Big Sleep, Vertigo, North by Northwest, The African Queen, Charade, Lawrence of Arabia, It's a Wonderful Life,* and *Some Like it Hot.* They all had identical wooden frames painted gold. The space was confusing to the girl.

She was brought to the center of the room facing the Council.

"You're curious about the posters," a woman seated at the center of the group said. She was thin with silver and black hair and appeared to be the oldest member of the council. She looked a lot like Rosita.

The girl nodded.

"They're all from Winthrop Holt's private collection," the woman said. "He identified these among his favorite movies in his Bunker 15C Journals. He was what they used to call a 'film buff'."

"Did you know Winthrop Holt?" the girl asked.

"None of us did," the woman answered. "He was before our

time. But his teachings on how to live inside the bunkers and outside after the reemergence have made the Ring of Winthrop community possible. His writings are our foundational texts. Even in death, he gives us strength."

The girl nodded again as if to communicate it all made sense to her, though she was still very confused.

"You have asked to speak to the Council of Chiefs," the woman said. "I am Chief Candice Winthrop. We comprise the senior leadership of the Winthrop Clan. We've been informed you're looking for someone. How does that concern us?"

"I'm looking for my father. He went in search of medical facilities to help my mother who was ill," the girl said, holding up the drawing of him. "Have you seen him?"

"I'm afraid I haven't," Chief Candice said. "Has anyone on the council seen or heard of someone who's description would match this illustration?"

The other chiefs shook their heads. Rosita walked around the long table and whispered something in Chief Candice's ear. They whispered back and forth to each other several times.

"Are you interested in becoming a Winthrop?" Chief Candice asked. "Rosita seems to think you might have something to offer, and she has good intuition in such matters."

"What does becoming a Winthrop entail?" the girl inquired.

"Passing a series of trials and examinations," Chief Candice said, "It would be challenging, physically and mentally. And while we are cautious and protective of our community, we like to think we are not entirely exclusive. However, should you deceive or bring harm to any member of our community, the penalty would be severe."

"Thank you for the opportunity," the girl said. "I'm honored, but I need to find my father before I settle down anywhere. Perhaps, after I've found out what happened to him, I'll reconsider the offer?"

Chief Candice looked to the other members of the counsel, who all gave her subtle deferring nods.

"That is acceptable to the council," Chief Candice said.

"May I show this drawing of my father around the village?" the girl asked.

"Rosita will accompany you to the end of our jurisdiction," Chief Candice said. "You may show it to anyone you see along the way, but no straying. The Ring of Winthrop is not open to the public."

"Thank you for the audience," the girl said.

Rosita took her out a different exit than they had used to enter the building. They walked a path between two rows of longhouses, obstructing a view of anything but the sides of buildings. Rosita stopped to retie her shoelaces next to a building. Screams came from within. They were sounds of agony and from more than one person. The girl could hear at least one voice begging them to stop.

"What's inside this building?" the girl asked.

"It's the brig," Rosita answered. "It's where we imprison and interrogate the enemies that we capture."

Rosita finished tying her laces. They continued walking. The girl knew they'd stopped for her benefit. To let her know what they'd do to her if she ever acted against them. She wondered if it was all an act to scare her. If inside the *brig* were just a handful of Rosita's comrades fabricating the sounds of torture. It didn't feel real to the girl.

When they were outside the gates, the girl said she could go on alone. Rosita told her the orders from the Council were to escort her to the end of the Winthrop Clan's land and those orders would be followed.

ESCORT SERVICE

The girl and Rosita were accompanied by eight sentries. At the end of the bare fields surrounding the ring fortress was a dense perimeter of woods, which operated as a secondary barrier of defense. Any large-scale assault would be slowed down by the thick woods and then the attacking forces would be exposed in the fields with nowhere to hide. As dangerous as the Phoenix warriors were in open skirmishes, it would be nearly impossible for them to come out victorious in an attack on the ring.

The small escort crew took an indirect route to avoid all the booby traps placed throughout the woods. Rosita and the sentries stopped talking after they left the fields because, among the trees and fallen leaves, it was easier to hear an ambush than it was to see one.

They'd nearly reached a clearing at the edge of the woods when they heard several clicking sounds from above, followed by war cries. Two Phoenix House warriors in their gray work suits fell from the trees above, each carrying two lit Molotov cocktails. One of them crashed onto Rosita, smashing both Molotovs as he hugged her. They were engulfed in flames, screaming as they struggled. The other Phoenix fell onto one of the sentries, smashing the

Moltovs on her victim, a mirror of her Phoenix brother's attack on Rosita. Rocks were thrown down from a third Phoenix in the trees as a small group came out of hiding and mounted an assault on the remaining sentries. The chaos was overwhelming.

Hare Bear and Biv emerged from behind some trees and put themselves between the girl and the battle. One of the Winthrop sentries broke away and ran back in the direction of the ring fortress. A Phoenix warrior pursued him.

"We're gonna come back for you, Maple," the Winthrop sentry yelled out as he ran away. "You'll regret this."

The sentry took a sudden turn and the Phoenix warrior stepped on a land mine, setting off two large explosions. After the smoke cleared and falling pieces of the warrior settled, the Winthrop sentry was too far away to catch.

The remaining members of the Phoenix hunting party turned towards the girl, Hare Bear, and Biv.

"I want to meet the Collage," the girl said.

"Why?" one of them asked. He had a transplanted nose and left hand. A large burn scar starting at the top of his left temple and ending at his jawline, and while the rest of them wore identical gray suits, his was sky blue, which the girl interpreted as a higher-ranking color.

"We want to join you," the girl answered. "Don't we?"

Hare Bear and Biv nodded in agreement, knowing it was their best option at the   moment.

"Why?" the Phoenix man asked.

"Because you're so powerful," she said, "and beautiful."

"Why should we believe you?" He asked.

"Did we fight against you during that battle?" She answered. "Did we try to run away?"

The Phoenix looked to the rest of his hunting party and took a moment to consider her answer.

"Do we pose a threat to you?" the girl asked. "Let's say you take us with you and the Collage decides not to believe us, what could we do? We're at your mercy."

"Ok," the Phoenix man said. "We'll take you back and let the Collage decide, but we're tying your hands behind your back. If you try anything, we'll peel the skin off your arms before we deliver you to the Collage."

"That seems reasonable and fair under the circumstances," the girl said. "I'm Maple."

"Yeah, I heard," he said. "I'm Eddie."

"This is Hare Bear and Biv," the girl said but Eddie had already turned away from her.

"Gather those two surviving Winthrops," Eddie said to two of his hunting party. He pointed two others toward the girl, Hare Bear, and Biv. "We're moving out in 40-Mississipi."

He began to count out loud.

"This arrangement doesn't seem fair at all," Hare Bear whispered in the girl's ear.

"No whispering," Eddie shouted. "5-Mississippi, 6-Mississipi."

The hunting party tied all their captives' hands behind their backs and then searched every nook and cranny of the four remaining unburned dead bodies, stripping them down for valuable goods and supplies, taking weapons, ammunition, tools, food, and so on. Everything but their clothes. This was all carried out systematically like they were field dressing a deer.

"39-Mississippi, 40-Mississippi," Eddie finished counting. "Let's roll out."

THE MOUTH OF THE PHOENIX

As they approached the Phoenix House, the girl noticed a couple dozen guards wearing green camouflage work suits keeping watch from tree stands spread out in what seemed a perimeter formation. The suits were the same style as the hunter's gray suits, which were zip-up coveralls. One of the guards made a bird-like call. Eddie responded with a different call, then they continued past the lookouts.

There was no defensive wall, but there were many more armed hunters and guards, and many more people overall, then there were inside the Ring of Winthrop. They walked by a few cabins and structures, but the architecture was sparser and smaller. A spacious clearing centered around a large stage, which was primarily used for ceremonial performances, rituals, sacrifices, rulings, and speeches. The animal pits were to the right of the stage with numbered signs staked next to each of them. The spinning carnival wheel deciding which pit the condemned would be thrown into was stationed between the stage and the pits.

The group was led to a hill in the center of it all with a large entrance to a tunnel at its base. The frame around the entrance was made of granite and carved into the shape of a fierce bird made up of parts from different birds. The head jutted out above the top of the entrance and large wings stretched down along the sides.

They walked through the entrance and down the tunnel, which ended at a large metal door. Two guards in gray overalls were stationed on either side of the door. Upon seeing Eddie, one of the guards entered a code on a wall mounted keypad, which unlocked the door allowing them to open it for the group. Through the door was an entrance chamber leading to another door, which Eddie unlocked using another keypad.

"Where are you taking us?" the girl asked.

"To see the Collage," Eddie said. "Eventually."

They were taken through another door labelled Waiting Room, which housed several small holding cells, each large enough for a single occupant. The doors were made of steel bars. Once they were locked in their cells, Eddie and his hunting party left the room, leaving a single guard sitting at a table to watch over them.

The girl could see Hare Bear in his cell across from her. He looked claustrophobic, pacing in what little space was provided, repeatedly raising his finger as if he were about to speak, then lowering his arm.

"Hare Bear," the girl beckoned.

He looked over to her.

"Relax," the girl said. "Everything will be okay. This is what we wanted. Deep breaths."

Hare Bear's nodding response looked like a flutter. He closed his eyes and started breathing deeply and slowly exhaling. Biv was in the cell next to Hare Bear, sitting cross-legged on top of their cot and rubbing their temples. They looked uncomfortable, but the girl didn't say anything because Biv seemed to have it under control.

"You fucking rat piece of shit," one of the captive Winthrop sentries cried out. "When Chief Candice gets her hands on you, and she will, she's gonna peel your skin from your body and then salt your bloody flesh. She'll keep you alive for days while she does it. You're afraid of these Phoenix freaks because you think they're more sadistic, but we're just as vicious. We just don't hide behind it like we're at a costume party."

The girl remained silent and watched Hare Bear, who was trying to ignore the disturbing imagery and focus on his breathing.

"Rosita was her daughter," the sentry said.

"I know," the girl said and closed her eyes to get some relief from the bright overhead lighting.

TO THE ALTAR, STAT

The girl woke up to Eddie shaking her, demanding she get up. A handful of gray suits were rousing everyone else from their cells. They were marched single file out of the holding room and down a long hallway. The Temple of Surgery was stenciled in large black serif lettering above a set of double doors they walked through, opening into a large circular space with several workstations and desks. Six sets of push doors were evenly spaced around the room with numbered signs: OR1, OR2, OR3, OR4, OR5, and OR6. The girl expected the space to be filled with icons and statues, murals depicting false sagas and illustrated mythologies of Phoenix House lore. But, besides the bird sculpture around the exterior entrance, the décor was institutional and sparse. Most of the objects they encountered were utilitarian in nature.

The Temple of Surgery staff all wore white coveralls, which were of the same cut and style as the other Phoenix suits. At least two-thirds of them had blood stains and spatter all over their suits. They were all very busy, talking over each other and never sitting still, as if existing in a never-ending emergency.

"What is this place?" Hare Bear whispered.

Biv looked at him, shaking their head with a nearly imperceptible furrow that screamed a thousand shut-the-fuck-ups.

Eddie waved one of the surgeons over and pointed out the two Winthrop sentries. The surgeon nodded, but gestured at the girl, Hare Bear, and Biv for clarification.

"Not yet," Eddie said.

As they were led back out into the hallway, surgeons forcibly strapped the Winthrop sentries onto gurneys, tightening the restraints until they could no longer move anything but their heads. The sentries cried out for help. The girl could hear them begging her for mercy after she'd been led out of the room and back down the long hallway. They promised no repercussions for her betrayal if she helped them, pleading that no one deserved this fate. She considered trying to help them because she agreed with the sentiment. This was no way to spend your last hours or, if you were unlucky, days or weeks. But the more they screamed for help, the more the girl realized how helpless their situation was and that, even if by miracle, she was able to free them and get them back to the Ring of Winthrop unharmed, she and her friends would be put down, executed publicly in memory of Rosita. She turned her thoughts to finding her father instead.

THE COLLAGE SPEAKS

The long hallway ended at another set of double doors with The Hall of the Collage stenciled above in the same font size and style as the black lettering for The Temple of Surgery. There were no extravagant fixtures around the entrance, just metal doors painted the same off white as the hallway walls. The two gray suits standing guard opened the doors for the group to enter.

They walked into a large chamber and were immediately greeted by a man in bright yellow coveralls. His sleeves were tailored short to display his transplants, which included two hands and a forearm. The skin tones were so drastically different, it seemed intentional, making him look fragmented. His own skin was pale and white. He had two different transplanted ears and the area around his mouth was swollen, but he kept his lips closed so no one could look inside his mouth.

"This is Maple," Eddie said. His body language was deferential to the man in the yellow suit. "She and her two friends want to join us. I've brought them to meet the Collage."

The man in the yellow walked to the girl to look her over, then sized up Hare Bear and Biv. He never spoke a word but looked at Eddie and nodded. He left through a door at the back of the chamber while Eddie led them to the center of the room. The only décor was a massive painting of a bird on the wall directly in front of them. It was not dissimilar to the bird sculpted around the exterior entrance to the bunker, yet another bird made up of many birds. Below the painting was a simple but elegant wooden podium.

The man in yellow reentered through the door at the back of the room. He was followed by four gray suits and then a man in scarlet red overalls—he was the Collage. The sleeves on his work suit were cut and tailored at the shoulders, exposing the entirety of his arms, which were not his own, but they matched each other. They were muscular and brown. The hands were from yet another donor with a lighter tone than the arms. His original skin was the same tone as the man in the yellow suit.

It was hard to decipher what work had been done to his face because the headdress he wore obscured everything above his mouth. A mask covering the upper half of his face was composed of the skins of different parts from different faces sewn together as a patchwork: swatches of forehead, two separate ears, two half-brows, two cheeks, two ears, and a nose. The mask was attached to a scalp constructed from three different heads, each with a different color and texture of long shoulder-length hair: thick blonde, curly red, and straight black. His eyes were bright red and looked artificial.

He walked over to the podium and took in the girl, Hare Bear, and Biv.

"Welcome to the Phoenix House," he said in a deep commanding voice. "I am the Collage."

"Bow down before him," Eddie demanded.

They all got down on one knee and kept their heads down, not knowing what was expected of them.

"Rise up," the Collage said to them, gesturing to the man in yellow. "Pardon my son's silence. Last week, he received a new tongue and it's still in the process of healing."

"That's okay," Hare Bear responded. "We don't mind."

"Do not speak unless the Collage asks you a question!" Eddied snapped at them.

"I understand that you wish to join us," the Collage said. He looked directly at the girl. "Why?"

"My family was slaughtered," the girl said. "They were slaughtered because they were weak. They were not made for this world and that's why they're dead. We want to join you because we want to be powerful. And we want to be part of something larger than ourselves."

"And why should we allow you to become part of our house?" the Collage asked.

"We're good hunters," the girl said, "and we've managed to make our way here to plead our case with you."

"With the help of the Winthrops," the Collage said.

"We're not members of that clan," she said. "It's just us three."

The Collage looked to Eddie for a confirmation of her claims.

"It was just Maple being escorted by the Winthrop group," Eddie said. "When the fighting began, the other two came out of nowhere like they'd been following the Winthrops in secret. They got between Maple and the bloodshed. Not one of them tried to help the Winthrops. They just watched us slaughter them."

The Collage made eye contact with the man in yellow, who responded with a facial expression communicating his skepticism.

"What if this is all a set-up? A ruse?" the Collage questioned. "What if this was the plan all along and the Winthrops you fought with had sacrificed their own lives to get some spies on the inside of the Phoenix House?"

"One of the dead was Rosita," Eddie said.

"Chief Candice's daughter?" the Collage asked.

"Yes," Eddie said. "She'd never sacrifice her own daughter. Rosita was being groomed to become Head Chief of the council after her mother. Rosita meant the world to her. War is coming. It might already be on its way."

"Get all of my kindred in place," the Collage commanded. "We must overwhelm them when they first enter our forest. That's where the war will be won, not on our doorstep. We must not allow them even a moment to acclimate to these surroundings."

"Yes, Collage," Eddie said.

"Do you trust them?" the Collage asked, gesturing his open hand towards the girl.

"No," Eddie said. "But I don't think they're with the Winthrops."

"Do you like them?" the Collage asked.

"Don't know yet," Eddie said.

"Time will tell," the Collage said, speaking to the girl. "For your first trial, each of you must hunt down and bring back a living donor, then I will decide which part of them will be transplanted onto you. From there you will be given a series of challenges and missions to complete after which my son and I will decide whether to offer you a place in our house."

"If you don't," Hare Bear asked.

"Then we'll wear you well," the Collage said with a satisfied smile. "In the meantime, we have a war upon us, which you played no small part in aggravating. But it has long been inevitable. Best to get it over with. You'll remain my guests in this house for the time being. Once the purging is complete, your trials may begin."

The Collage and the man in yellow left the chamber.

FOUR-STAR ACCOMMODATIONS

The Girl, Hare Bear, and Biv were not taken back to the holding cells. Instead, they were given a two-bedroom suite with an open-plan common area. The space was equipped with an entertainment center, a small kitchen with a stocked pantry, running water, electricity, a bathroom, a long couch, a table with chairs, and a modest library of books. It was the nicest place any of them had ever stayed. Being offered these luxuries felt strange under the circumstances, but it was hard not to indulge in them.

"What's your plan, Maple?" Hare Bear asked as he walked around the room opening every drawer, inspecting everything, and testing objects and surfaces to find out what moved and didn't move, what was hidden and what was just as it appeared to be.

"The plan is to find my father," she responded.

"But how?" he inquired.

"I'm going to ask the Collage to give us a tour of the Phoenix House facilities," she said.

"Why would he do that?" Hare Bear asked.

"He might not trust us," the girl said, "but I think he likes us and, more importantly, he doesn't see us as a threat. A man like him gets a certain satisfaction out of being able to lay all his cards on the table and still win."

"What do we do while we wait?" he asked.

"Enjoy everything this place has to offer while it's available to us," the girl said. She traced her finger along a shelf of books as she read the titles on the bindings, which were in no particular order: *The Iliad* by Homer, *Murder on the Orient Express* by Agatha Christie, *The Complete Works of Shakespeare*, *Congo* by Michael Crichton, *Beloved* by Toni Morrison, *Middlemarch* by George Eliot, *Cujo* by Stephen King, *Native Son* by Richard Wright, *The Firm* by John Grisham, *The Vampire Lestat* by Anne Rice, *Leaves of Grass* by Walt Whitman, *To the Lighthouse* by Virginia Woolf. She stopped at a copy of *The Adventures of Sherlock Holmes* by Sir Arthur Conan Doyle and took it off the shelf. Her mother used to read to her from a different Sherlock Holmes book called *The Hound of the Baskervilles*. It had been one of her favorites, even when it scared her as a child. She sat cozily at one end of the couch and opened the book.

"You know," the girl said, pausing to look around the suite, "amid all this madness, they kind of have their shit together."

"They butcher people into little pieces," Biv responded, "selecting them at random, then wearing their victims' body parts like costumes."

"I'm not defending them," the girl said, "and I'm not saying they're in their right mind. It's just that there's something about this place that's systematically preserved. It's civic and organized. It's not what I expected."

"Do you think this food is safe to eat?" Hare Bear interjected.

"Yes," Biv said. "I'm pretty sure they want you healthy when they start slicing you up."

"Oh," Hare Bear responded. He let it sink in, then spread some lard on a piece of bread and devoured it. "This is really tasty though."

The girl began reading the first story in the collection, "A Scandal in Bohemia." Biv left the common room, sat on one of the beds, and rubbed their temples. Hare Bear spread lard on another chunk of bread and poured himself a glass of water as he searched through the rest of the kitchen to see what else there was to eat.

THE GRAND TOUR

They walked around the facility. The Collage allowed the girl to walk side-by-side with him while the man in yellow, Hare Bear, Biv, and four gray suits followed behind. The Collage liked the girl and had already decided he wanted her to join his house, though he would keep that to himself until she'd gone through the trials successfully and it was made official. Perhaps he might even mate with her someday, he thought. Their offspring would be formidable.

The girl noticed his fondness. The tour took some time. The facility was made up of four stories, each of which was massive. She imagined they must have been incredibly wealthy before the bunkers. Still, it seemed too small to house all its members.

"Is there room for all of you here?" the girl asked.

"To sleep?" the Collage countered. "No, and that's why we operate on six-hour shifts. There's never more than one-fourth of us sleeping at a time. Most of us share living quarters. It's similar to the way old submarine crews utilized tight quarters when they were out to sea for months at a time."

"Do *you* share living quarters?" the girl asked.

"No," he said with a smile. "I'm the captain."

His smile made the girl feel sick, but she couldn't ignore any edge or advantage handed over so easily to her. She smiled back. Thus far, they'd only been shown living quarters, the kitchen, the main dining room, and common recreational spaces like the movie theater, game room, and pub. The girl couldn't think of a roundabout way to ask where all the living donors were being held captive without appearing to have an agenda unrelated to joining the Phoenix House.

Eddie walked up to the Collage, interrupting the tour, just as they walked through a set of double doors with The Temple of Surgery stenciled above, but it was not the same doorway they'd walked though earlier.

"Sir," Eddie said. "All our forces are in position. A scouting group returned and confirmed the Winthrops are approaching. By their reckoning, it's almost the entire Winthrop army."

"Good," the Collage responded. "We'll end it today. This has been a long time coming. It's time for a new chapter of the Phoenix House. We will be reborn today and rise from the ashes unchallenged. The world will be ours."

The girl tried to ignore all the megalomania as she scanned the hallway and noticed a door with the words Surgical Recovery stenciled above.

"We will be victorious, Collage," Eddie said, not sounding as confident as his leader. "It will be a day of legend. I need to return to the battlefront. Would you like me to send a unit of hunters back to help protect the house?"

"No," the Collage responded. "I think we can handle things here. If you see Chief Candice, take her out first. It will throw them off. They'll be headless without her."

"A wise strategy, sir," Eddie affirmed. He signaled with an index finger to the three hunters in camouflage coveralls who had accompanied him, and they followed him out.

"Could we see the Surgical Recovery wing next?" the girl asked.

The man in yellow looked at his father and shook his head emphatically. It was apparent he had a lot to say and was desperate to speak again.

"Why?" asked the Collage.

"I want to see the entire process," the girl said. "The artistry is in the craft as much as the final product."

"Well put," the Collage said.

"If you prefer to wait," the girl said, looking at both father and son, "we have no objections. I was only asking."

"We have nothing to hide," the Collage said. "No big secrets will be revealed if you walk through that door. The words above are self-explanatory. Pardon my son, he's only being protective of me, for which I am grateful."

He patted his son on the back and smiled to reassure him they were in control of the situation. He also wanted to use this as an opportunity to see how the girl, Hare Bear, and Biv would react to seeing living donors in various stages of surgical removal. It would be their first trial. He felt no threat to his empire, which had sheltered and protected him away from the rest of the world for years.

The Collage opened the door and waved for the girl to go first.

DONOR GALLERY

The surgical recovery unit had a wide central path for foot traffic and was lined with enclosures, eight on each side. Each enclosure had a hospital bed, medical equipment for monitoring vitals, an adjustable tray table with wheels for eating, and a sitting chair. The facing walls were made of glass so visitors could observe everything. Large plexiglass windows were centered on the walls between enclosures to allow donors to see the state each other was in. Designed to be as much a viewing room as it was a medical care unit, it seemed equal parts recovery ward, zoo, and museum.

Donors were in varying states of anatomical removal. The first couple donors they saw had undergone only one removal so far, a hand from one and a foot from the other. As they walked further along the enclosures, the number and severity of removals from each donor grew. The girl realized this was intentional. The progression was theater.

They stopped for at least one minute at each enclosure to observe the inhabitant while a surgeon described each removal procedure more like a tour guide than a doctor doing rounds. There were framed photos hanging on the walls of every enclosure of the donor's transplanted body part on its recipient, one photo for each donation. For older donations, updated photos displayed the recipient with a fully healed and operational transplant. The photos of recent donations were taken in the post-operative recovery unit for recipients while the transplant wounds were still healing. The tour surgeon discussed the recipients and how their transplants have enlightened them.

"Where do the donors go after they've recovered from surgery?" the girl asked.

The surgeon, who himself had a transplanted left hand and right ear, looked to his superiors for permission to answer her question. The Collage nodded in affirmation.

"Once they've recovered," the surgeon answered, "they begin preparations for their next donation."

"There's no other space where they're kept?" the girl asked.

"No," the surgeon said. "They live here until their philanthropy is complete."

The girl was even more terrified for her father. With only six enclosures left ahead of them, she wasn't sure what to hope for.

"Is everything okay?" asked the Collage, who was paying close attention to her reactions.

"Yes," the girl said. "This is all so overwhelming and sublime. I'm feeling a lot of intense emotions right now."

"Is that a good thing?" the Collage asked.

"Oh yes," she said. "It's everything I'd hoped it would be and more."

"Wonderful," the Collage said, pleased with her responses.

Inside the next enclosure was the girl's father. The first thing she noticed was that his right hand was missing, which was upsetting, but she couldn't immediately identify any other removals. As much as she was relieved, she was confused. If the progression of enclosures was consistent, he should have at least one more removal.

Her father ran up to the glass the moment he recognized her. He was too disoriented and excited to consider the consequences of revealing their connection. When he opened his mouth, the first thing the girl noticed was the absence, the emptiness inside his mouth. His tongue had been removed. She knew immediately it had been given to the man in yellow.

Before the Collage could speak and command his security detail to attack, the girl had removed the large hunting knife from the man in yellow's sheath and knocked him over the head with the metal butt of his own weapon, leaving him stunned on the ground. She stabbed the surgeon three times in the abdomen as she made her way over to the Collage. The gray suits ignored Hare Bear and Biv as they went to stop her. Hare Bear took out three by himself, grabbing a baseball bat from one and using it against them all. He was too fast and strong for them. Biv snuck up behind the last gray suit, took his pistol from its holster, and shot him twice in the chest. He'd bragged earlier about how the gun was a trophy from a Winthrop ambush he'd been part of.

When the girl reached the Collage she kneed him in the gut and pulled his headdress off. Underneath the mask was a well-groomed head and face. No transplanted facial features, just a middle-aged man with some graying at the temples who took good care of himself. He was well-fed and rested. No bags under his eyes. No dirt under his fingernails. As if he'd been living in a different world all this time.

The girl had no use for words with him and slit his throat before he had a chance to ask for mercy. She walked back over to the man in yellow, who was being restrained by Hare Bear.

"That's my father's tongue," she said, then reached in his mouth and tore it out. She returned to her father's enclosure and opened the door. They embraced and both started crying. Hare Bear snapped the man in yellow's neck.

HOUSECLEANING

In the aftermath of the recovery unit skirmish, the girl and her friends realized they would not only have to contend with any Phoenixes left in the facility, but the war going on in the surrounding woods. Regardless of who came out of the battle triumphant, the three of them would be considered enemies of the victor. Hare Bear was spiraling into a terrible anxiety attack. The girl was trying to deal with her father, who'd just found out his wife had passed away, while trying to come up with a solution to their situation. Biv was rubbing their temples.

"I'll handle it," Biv said.

"What do you mean?" Hare Bear asked. "How?"

"I need you two to take control of this facility and deal with anyone who's still here," they said. "I'll handle the situation outside."

"That's crazy," Hare Bear said. "Have you lost your mind?"

"I'll be fine," Biv said. "But once I leave and close the front door to the Phoenix House, you must keep it closed until I return. Don't let anyone leave."

Hare Bear moved towards Biv to stop them, but the girl grabbed him by the shirt.

"Let them go," she said. "They seem to have a plan. Do you have a plan?"

THE BATTLE IN THE WOODS

Biv left the bunker and entered the woods. They walked for a little over a quarter mile until they reached the fringe of the battle. It started with scattered corpses and a few smaller fights. One or two Winthrop Clan soldiers making their way to the Phoenix House going up against the last line of gray suits.

Biv took their time, stealthily, to avoid being detected. They were looking for the heart of the battle.

It became increasingly more difficult to go unnoticed. They had to move swiftly. The deeper they went into the battle, the thicker the woods were with bodies, living and dead. Blood was everywhere. On the trees. Staining the forest floor. The air smelled of gunpowder. All they could hear was screaming. There were different screams. Some filled with rage. Some sounded victorious. Some were made in agony. Others pleaded for them to give in and concede. Biv stopped for a moment to rub their temples.

The slaughter had taken over the landscape. It was hard to decipher who was winning. The body count didn't appear to favor one group over the other. Body parts of all shapes and sizes were laying everywhere. The screaming was more intense the closer they got to the center of the battle.

When they'd been traversing a thick soup of annihilation for what seemed a half mile, Biv saw Eddie leading a group against a massive horde of Winthrop soldiers. Their eyes met.

The screaming got worse. Hundreds of screams were coming at them from every direction. Millions of voices screamed inside their head. Biv looked around and then, overcome, vomited on the ground. Once they'd wiped their mouth and composed themselves, they lifted the bronze pendant to their lips and blew. A few blood-soaked warriors stopped their fighting when they heard the whistle's soft tone. Eddie looked directly at Biv, bewildered by their actions.

The earth was unleashed and ate them all, swallowing both armies into the dirt. Less than two minutes later, there was no one left to fight the battle. Biv was alone in the woods.

AFTER THE WHISTLE

When Biv returned to the Phoenix House, they didn't speak to anyone for three days, spending time alone in one of the suites or outside away from others. The girl noticed Biv had stopped rubbing their temples. But, while the headaches had gone away, something else had changed.

The girl and Hare Bear cleared the bodies out of the Phoenix House bunker. All told, there were maybe twenty to carry out and bury. Very few Phoenixes had stayed behind in the facility during the battle. Most of the surgical staff surrendered and were locked in holding cells.

"What's next?" Hare Bear asked the girl as they finished patting the dirt over the last grave with their shovels.

"We make a home for ourselves," the girl answered. "Either here or at the Ring of Winthrop. Maybe both."

"Here?" Hare Bear asked. "Even after everything."

"We'll see," she said. "I don't think we'll ever find better facilities, though we still haven't had a tour of the Winthrop bunker. Of course, wherever we choose to settle, we'll have to redecorate. Make it ours. What do you think?"

"I'll make do," Hare Bear responded. "I'm good at adjusting

to whatever needs adjusting to, plus it's better having people than being alone. How's your father?"

"He's alive," she said, "and that'll have to be enough for now."

"How are you?" he asked.

"Not as angry," the girl said. "But just as sad."

They left the unmarked mounds of dirt and returned to the bunker. They tended to the surviving donors and began the long process of purging the facility of materials characteristically linked to the Phoenix House.

When they were finished, they built a huge bonfire in the middle of a field and gradually burned all the coveralls they'd found stored in the bunker. It took a day to burn them all. The surviving donors insisted they work systematically, burning one color at a time. They started with the grays, then green camouflage, the surgical whites, the sky blues, the man in yellow's yellows, and ending with the sleeveless scarlet reds of the Collage. They all watched until every little piece of fabric was burned to ash.

HOWLING AT THE NEW MOON

Months later, a new community had been established. Geographically, it was made up of the Ring of Winthrop and the former Phoenix House territories combined. The community was named Wolf's Head in honor of the girl's mother.

The girl acted as overseer of the community and its lands with the help of Hare Bear and Biv. They were often known to emphasize these were caretaking roles and not those of superiors looking down on their subjects.

Wolf's Head was open to those who were willing to respect the rules of the community and offer their equal labor to help all members remain healthy and thrive. This hospitality was denied to those who would not agree to their terms.

The four members of the Winthrop council of chiefs who'd stayed behind during the battle protested these structural changes and refused to recognize the new community. They were asked to leave, and they obliged.

The remaining members of the Winthrop clan voluntarily joined Wolf's Head. They were made up of the clan's farmers, doctors, nurses, schoolteachers, builders, and children. When asked by the surviving Winthrops what had happened in the woods and where all their soldiers had gone, their fathers and mothers and sisters and brothers and sons and daughters, the girl responded she didn't know and explained that they'd been in the Phoenix House during the battle and only knew for sure the fates of the Collage and those who'd stayed behind with him. She assured them that when they explored the woods for survivors after the battle, there were some corpses scattered around, but most of the warriors from both sides had disappeared, leaving behind only some weapons and their blood spattered on tree trunks and foliage. This was a partial truth. The girl didn't know exactly what transpired in the woods, but she did withhold the detail of Biv being present during the battle.

The girl and Hare Bear split their time between both settlements. Biv dwelled mostly on the former Phoenix House land where there were fewer people. They built a cabin not too far from the bunker entrance, but isolated enough to be a place where they could go to get away from everyone and be alone.

Three packs of wild Armstrong dogs moved into the Wolf's Head lands. Initially, there were some skirmishes suggesting the packs would all go to war with each other to mark their dominance over the territory. One alpha and one pack to rule the rest. If the physical remains of these smaller incidents were any indication, it would have been a relentless and vicious war. The people of Wolf's Head started feeding the dogs. They'd bring out enough food for all, setting it on the same spot at the same time every day, creating a routine. Gradually, the dogs bonded with the people, usually a dog would attach itself to a specific person and become a peripheral member of their person's family. Overtime, the separate packs disbanded, and the dogs became one with the community.

The dogs wandered the land, scaring off larger predators and hunting game. Some of the dogs slept in houses. Some preferred finding their own dens. But they all fed together on what was given to them by the people and what they'd caught for themselves. One runt of a litter took to Emmett when he was making a weekly delivery. After two more visits, the bond had grown so strong between them the puppy went to live with the Salt-maker and his family on the coast, spending days running around the evaporation ponds and chasing seagulls.

The rest of the dogs stayed in Wolf's Head. They grew in numbers. Dozens of them patrolled the land, protecting their territory. Travelers were wary of the community. Word spread of the dogs and the great battle between the Winthrop Clan and the Phoenix House. Some claimed the earth swallowed them all. Others refused to believe such nonsense. Still, some believed the land was haunted. Stories were told around campfires at Holyoke, warning of hungry shadows and waves of teeth prowling the woods of Wolf's Head as if hellhounds had risen from the underworld and possessed the land, spattering the underbrush, leaving none but the dead in their path.

But these wild claims were just fodder for folk tales and reckless conspiracy theories. The dogs were no demons. They were real. They were descendants of a celebrity. Survivors of apocalypse. Guardians of the new world. They were unbound by their artificial beginnings. They were better than their creators.

Long live *Canis Armstrongus*.

ACKNOWLEDGMENTS

I'd like to thank Diane Goettel and Yvonne C. Garrett for selecting *Habitat* for Black Lawrence Press. And to Diane for all the guidance and hard work through every step of this process. Nina Smilow for her thorough and incisive editing. Kit Frick for everything she's done to prepare this book for publication. Ani Jones for all their work on publicity and event planning. Zoe Norvell for her incredible cover and interior design and Jenna Barton (a.k.a. Dappermouth) for her piece "Ghost Summer," which serves as perfect cover art for *Habitat*.

My deep gratitude to Josh Bell, Kristian Macaron, Neel Mukherjee, Eric Smith, Josh White, Greg Whitmore, and my 2nd Sunday Sci-Fi Crew (Josephine Anstey, Raquel Baker, Wongoon Cha, Cathy Davidson, Jess Erion, & Margaret Rhee) who have each probably read this book almost as much as I have, for their invaluable feedback, brainstorming, and support.

Thanks to Jeff Gould for his generous help navigating the world of permissions, and to Jon Chaiim McConnell for his advice on getting a first book published.

Thanks to the journals and editors who have published pieces from *Habitat*: Justin Taylor and Minna Zallman Proctor at *The Literary Review* for publishing "Potluck Barbecue," and to Justin for his support and encouragement of my writing. Christina Thompson and Chloe Garcia Roberts at *The Harvard Review*, with gratitude to

Christina for her work editing "The Man Who Knew The Collage."
Laura van den Berg for her generosity and for selecting "Protected
Land" to be published in *West Branch*.

To Gabriella Gage, Jorie Graham, Amelia Klein, Nancy Mendoza,
Mark Poirier, Pete Rudolph, Jackie Ryan-Rudolph, Namwali Ser-
pell, TJ Stanehart, Mike Vazquez, Henry Vega-Ortiz, and Virocode
(Andrea Mancuso & Peter D'Auria) for their feedback and support
of this book.

A very special thanks to Mako Yoshikawa for her enduring men-
torship and friendship.

To my Buffalonians, Druidians, Emersonians, Movie-nighters,
Williams Roasticonians, and all my beloved friends and family—
thank you!

To my mother, Mary, and my father, Bob, for everything.

To Stella for all the endless joy, curiosity, and inspiration you bring
me; I learn from you every day. And to Sarah, my first reader, best
friend, co-pilot, partner-in-crime, and everything else, including
the kitchen sink. I love you both...so much.

CASE Q. KERNS is a writer from Buffalo, NY. He received a degree in Cinema & Photography from Ithaca College and an MFA from Emerson College where he served as fiction editor for the literary journal Redivider. His work has appeared in *The Literary Review*, *The Harvard Review*, and *West Branch*. *Habitat* is his debut novel. He lives in Massachusetts with his family.